Shadowy Passions Unleashed

The Incubus' Passion 1

Shadowy Passions Unleashed

The Incubus' Passion 1

by

Reed James

Naughty Ladies Publications

Cover Photo © Vadymvdrobot | Depositphotos.com

Logo © Anton Brand | Dreamstime.com

Cover Design by Amber Naralim

Naughty Ladies Publications

www.NaughtyLadiesPublications.com

ISBN-13: 9781794299351

Table of Contents

Chapter One: Dream Lover

Kyrie Hope

My feet were killing me as I trudged up the outside stairs of my apartment building in my heeled boots. The Coat of Arms Apartments weren't the worst in the city, but they weren't as good as I'd like. It was the best I could afford on my wages and tips working as a bartender. It was close to my job, The Green Eye Delight, a popular club. A short walk was important at three in the morning. I was always tense coming home, my shoulders hunched, so aware of anything that could be lurking in the shadows.

Like *him*.

I pushed my bastard ex out of my thoughts as I fumbled to get my keys out of my purse. I found them as I reached the well-lit walkway that lined the second floor of the building. My door was three down, apartment 211. The jingling of my keys lifted the head of the black cat sitting on my doormat.

I blinked as her green, slitted eyes met mine. I frowned at the cat, wondering why she was sleeping on my doormat. She rose with that feline grace, back arching as her mouth opened in a slow yawn. I considered the cat as she faced me, eyes unblinking. She sat down on her haunches, her tail flicking behind her. She was all black, almost a shadow even beneath the light shining above my door.

"Well, hi there," I said, my voice full of the fake-brightness I used when tending bar. I would never let my patrons know I was tired. I was a professional.

The cat flicked her ears.

"Guess I got a comfy welcome mat, huh?" I asked, moving towards her.

I was surprised that the cat didn't bolt. There was nothing skittish about her pose. She held her ground, forcing me to move carefully so I didn't step on her twitching tail as I positioned myself in front of my door. To my shock, she rubbed her whiskered cheek against my skinny jeans, the whisking sound of her fur on denim filling the early morning air.

"Aren't you a friendly thing?" I said as my key clicked home into the deadbolt lock. "Are you one of my neighbor's?" I hadn't got a chance to know anyone else in the three weeks I'd lived here. I was busy working, trying to survive. I wasn't here to make friends. I was here to...

A shiver ran down my spine. I glanced over my shoulders, searching the shadows of the courtyard. I felt like someone was watching me. A quick scan revealed nothing. I shook my head again, knowing it was just my paranoia. Tyrone had no idea where I was.

I'd left everything behind.

I opened my door and, before I could stop her, the cat darted inside. I groaned, stumbling in after her, not in the mood for this. The cat hopped up onto my couch, curled up into a ball, and rested her muzzle on her front paws. Her tail half-dangled over the side, her fur standing out against the beige cushion. It was a little faded with age, but the couch was a good buy I'd found at the local thrift store. It matched the rest of my small living room.

That wasn't an easy feat when you prowled second-hand stores to decorate.

I was proud of the life I was building here. It wasn't what I expected when I was that bright-eyed eighteen-year-old girl heading off to college. Nearly six years had changed a lot. I had a fresh start, a chance to do things better.

To not make that mistake again...

You'd think a year of moving around would ease that tension at the base of my spine.

"Come on," I said, pointing at my open front door. "You can't stay here, cat."

She purred. That deep, rumbling sound rose from her. Her green eyes closed. I let out a sigh, tired. I just wanted to go to bed. I pushed at her side, trying to nudge her off the couch.

She kept purring.

My push turned into a stroke somehow as I marveled at how soft and warm her fur was. She felt like silk. I petted her, loving the feel of her beneath my fingers. Her purrs grew louder, filling my empty living room with life. A smile crossed my lips as my fingers slid up between her ears, scratching them. The triangular points twitched. Her tail flicked from side to side.

"Fine," I said, too tired to deal with this. "You stay the night, but you better not make a mess or claw my furniture."

The cat's green eyes opened with a lazy glide. Our gazes met, and I almost felt like she understood my words. Then they closed, and she drifted off into feline sleep.

I shut my front door, locked the deadbolt, then took off my heeled boots, sighing in relief. I stumbled through my living room to the short hallway that led to my bedroom and the small bathroom. I forced myself to remove my makeup. No matter how tired I was, I wouldn't let myself fall asleep like that.

Stripped of foundation, lipstick, eye shadow, and blush, with the faint scent of rubbing alcohol lingering around me, I tottered to my bedroom. I pulled off my halter top and removed my bra. My round breasts jiggled, still firm at twenty-four. My coppery red hair, which I considered to be my best feature, swayed about my shoulders as I wiggled out of my skinny jeans. Panties were off next, then I was drawing on my nightgown before I crawled into my bed.

I had to work again tomorrow. Ten hour shift.

The moment my head hit the pillows, I was out. I fell into

dreams.

I drifted through nonsense for a while, those abstract imaginations that flowed from one impossible thing that you just accept as normal to another. The type of dreams that left only the barest impressions upon your thoughts when you woke up.

And then something real entered the dreams. Something solid.

Heat quivered through me. It galvanized my loins, my pussy growing wet as I opened eyes to gaze upon him.

Not Tyrone, my abusive ex, but that dark, handsome man I saw flirting with all the women at the club tonight. He had the look of a Frenchman, brooding and passionate. Shaggy, near-black hair fell about a broad face, those heavy brows and soulful eyes melting every pair of panties in the bar.

Blue eyes. Deep and mesmerizing. The type of eyes you could just stare into for eternity.

When I first saw him enter, I thought he was cut straight off the cover of a romance novel. He stood tall and broad shouldered; a commanding presence that demanded the attention of everyone in the club. Dancers grinding together paused to glance in his direction, the women melting at the sight of him, the men scowling at the competition. He didn't have a swagger about him, but a confidence to his stride. He was a man who knew just the effect he had on women.

His eyes were hungry, hunting.

He didn't dress with extravagance like some of the peacocks who strutted around trying to attract the hens. No silk blazers or gold Rolexes. He was almost blue-collar in his simplicity. Jeans that fit his muscular thighs and hugged the firm, toned shape of his ass. A white t-shirt that clung to his sculpted pecs and rippling abs. He wore a leather jacket that completed the look, almost like a bomber jacket, dark as him, intriguing.

I remembered when he glanced at me tending bar, his eyes kindling at the sight of me. My nipples had puckered, the heat swelling my pussy. My coworker, Cyndi, had cooed in delight, *"Oh, my God, I'm creaming my panties just looking at him, Kyrie."*

Cyndi always was an outrageous gossip. Always glancing at the patrons of the club and pointing out hot guys, and the occasional sexy girl, to me. She was always talking about what she'd do with them. She was fun and flirty and open. When there was no one buying drinks, we'd chat about this or that girl's outfit, how that girl's purse didn't match her dress, that those shoes didn't go with that skirt, things like that.

She was always noticing.

Now in my dream, I was noticing *him*.

Those eyes stared at me like they had at the bar, drinking me in. He was at the door, not the door to my apartment, but somewhere else. He was so close to me I could feel the heat washing off his body. I could smell the leather of his jacket. There was another musk beneath it, that manly scent. He didn't wear cologne; didn't need it.

My thighs pressed together as that liquid warmth swelled in me. An ache formed at the tips of both my breasts, my body shivering in the long t-shirt I wore.

"I wasn't sure if you'd take me up on my invitation," I purred, my voice huskier than normal. A smoky contralto. I stood before my open apartment door, staring at him filling the portal.

"Well, it was such a welcoming invite," the man said, his eyes flicking up and down my body. "You promised... such interesting delights."

"With all those other women around you..." I shuddered. "I didn't think you'd even notice me. You were looking at *her* all night."

"But I'm looking at you, now." He reached through the doorway to cup my cheek. His fingers were warm, rough. His thumb rubbed across my chin, brushing my lower lip.

I quivered. An excited rush of heat boiled out of my pussy. I squeezed my thighs together, loving this dream. It felt so real.

When his thumb swept up to my lips, I didn't hesitate to suck him in. My cheeks hollowed as he worked his fat digit in and out of my mouth. My tongue caressed the end, tasting him. I groaned, such a wanton sound. He made me feel so womanly.

So desired.

His blue eyes sparkled, deep and intense. He slipped into my apartment almost like a shadow, the door closing behind him as his other hand slid around my hip to my lower back. Then he was cupping my ass, pulling me to him as his eyes held mine. My breasts pressed against his chest, feeling the strength of him through his white t-shirt. My nipples throbbed. I wished our clothing wasn't in the way so I could *feel* him against me.

My panties were soaked with my excitement.

My hands quivered, and then they were slipping beneath his jacket to feel the hard strength of his muscles. My fingernails scratched at his shirt. I tugged and pulled, untucking his shirt out of his jeans so I could reach beneath and touch his warmth directly.

I moaned around his thumb.

"You're just brimming with it," he groaned. "That wonderful ache. You were so envious of *her*, weren't you?"

I moaned and whimpered, not sure who this *her* was. I didn't care right now. He was here with me. He had come to *my* dream.

"It was you I wanted all night," he continued, his voice a deep, rumbling delight. It was soothing and passionate all at the same time, stoking the fires between my thighs and making me whimper.

He pulled his thumb from my mouth and claimed my lips with his before I could utter a word. His tongue thrust into my mouth as he kissed me with such passion, his hand squeezing me through my long t-shirt. He pulled me tight against him, letting me feel his passion through his jeans. A quiver ran through me. He was hung.

I hadn't had many lovers, especially not with three years spent as that bastard's girlfriend. This man—this masculine god poured into rock-hard flesh—put them all to shame.

I clutched him, my hands sliding higher and higher up his back beneath his t-shirt. My fingernails clawed at him as he awakened such passions in me.

How long had it been since I'd been with a man? Months? I was so busy trying to survive.

I kissed him back with such hunger, his tongue dueling with

mine as he pressed me back into the living room. I let him guide me. Control me. I felt like putty in his strong hands. One kneaded my rump while the other rubbed up and down my supple back. My nipples ached and throbbed against the cotton of my t-shirt. I felt his strength through our clothing. I wanted to be naked. My nightshirt itched at me. Clung to me. I needed it off of me.

I whimpered.

As if he understood, his hands shifted. They seized the hem of my long t-shirt and pulled it up my body. I broke from his embrace and took a breathless step back as he drew the cloth higher and higher. It passed my upper thighs then revealed the dark-red panties I wore.

I'd never seen this pair before. They were adorned with black lace around the waistband; cut narrow as it plunged down to cup my pussy. A sensual delight worn for a lover.

For him.

He dragged up my long t-shirt until he reached my breasts. His grin grew as he lifted my top higher so my tits spilled out. Not the round, firm ones I was used to, but larger ones. Soft and pillowy, with a heavy feel to them. My nipples were fat and dark-red, not my smaller, pink nubs.

I shivered. This dream was so strange. It felt so real, and yet so alien.

I groaned as I lifted my arms high, letting him pull the t-shirt off my body. My hair spilled around my shoulders. I caught a glimpse of brown strands, not my fiery red.

Who was I in this dream?

His hands engulfed my breasts, squeezing these large, soft mounds. His fingers were able to dig into them deeper than they would with my own. It was such a wild treat to have tits as big as my friend Cyndi's.

Wasn't there a brunette who showed up at the club tonight? A busty girl who was swaying on the dance floor and trying to catch this hunk's attention all night.

Was I her?

"These breasts," groaned the man, blue eyes deep as the ocean.

He pressed his face between them, the shadow of his whiskers rough against my sensitive flesh. I quivered, glad he enjoyed my tits. This was *my* body for the dream. I took such pride in the lust I inspired in him.

He squeezed and kneaded my breasts, digging his fingers into my flesh. I groaned as he rubbed his face back and forth between my heavy tits. His fingers swept up to find my fat nipples, pinching and rolling them. They were so sensitive, shooting delight straight down to my pussy. I whimpered, trembling. My poor panties were struggling to soak up all the passion flooding out of me.

"Yes," I whimpered, aching to express the emotions building in me. "Your touch... Oh, yes, your touch."

"I want to worship these breasts all night," groaned the man. He squeezed my tits around his face, whiskers rasping against my sensitive flesh. His blue eyes stared up at me from their valley. "To worship them. They are the breasts of a goddess."

Such joy quivered through me. This god thought *I* was worthy of worship.

His lips kissed and nuzzled and sucked at the inner swell of my tits. He climbed up my right breast, kissing higher and higher, reaching towards my aching nipple. I groaned as his lips drew near the edge of my areola.

I quivered as he engulfed my nipple. He sucked it into his hungry mouth, cheeks hollowing as he worshiped me. My pussy clenched and my entire body shuddered. His mouth was so warm about my nub, his lips so hungry. He squeezed and kneaded both my tits as he sucked and worshiped me.

"I wanted this all night," I moaned.

It was the truth. The moment I laid eyes on him when he strolled in, I wanted him. Like every other woman at the club, my friend included, I had ached for his attention. Every time he glanced at me, I trembled. I felt his eyes caressing me.

Now he touched me for real.

I loved this dream.

His mouth popped off my right nipple. His hot lips kissed down into the valley of my breasts again, his whiskered face rasping against my silky flesh. Then he climbed up my left breast, approaching that aching pinnacle. I quivered, gasped.

He engulfed my nipple.

"Oh, I'm so glad you chose me," I moaned. He sucked with that fervent hunger. "Me!"

His lips popped off my nipple as he growled, "How could I choose anyone else *but* you? You're my goddess. My muse. You've inspired me."

He fell to his knees before me. His fingers hooked the waistband of my dark-red panties. With a single jerk, he yanked. I felt the pinch at my waist as the cloth dug into my flesh before the dainty garment tore free. He wrenched the panties from me and threw the scrap to the ground. He was strong. So powerful.

I was laid bare before him, my pussy exposed. He kissed my pudenda then nuzzled down the thin line of brown hair leading to the shaved folds of my snatch. I hadn't been shaved since *him*.

I pushed thoughts of Tyrone away. I wouldn't think about that bastard now. Not when I had the man feasting on me. I felt so womanly as the stranger, the hunk, kissed down my landing strip to my shaved vulva. My thighs parted to let him have access to my womanhood.

My molten sex.

His lips nuzzled at the top folds of my pussy. His tongue flicked through my labia, caressing my clit already peeking out of its hood. He groaned in delight, savoring the flavor of my passion. I quivered, my large breasts swaying with my every movement. His hand slid around, grabbing my rump. He gripped me tight as he worshiped my pussy.

He feasted on my passion.

His blue eyes stared up at me, devouring my soul while he ate my snatch. His tongue churned through my folds, caressing my labia. My clit. He touched every bit of me with his agile tongue. He knew how to please a woman.

I could see it in his eyes, a dark hunger that was savoring the bliss of eating me out. He wanted to love me. To make me explode.

My hands shot down to grip his hair. I gasped, spotting the snarling tiger tattooed on my inner right forearm. This was definitely not my body, but that busty brunette's. I would never mar my perfect flesh with a tattoo.

I held his thick mane of hair as the pleasure rippled through my body. I ground on him, whimpering delight as every stroke of his tongue built my orgasm. It grew and grew inside of me, his tongue caressing my petals. His fingers dug into my rump, holding me against his hungry mouth while his tongue jammed deep inside of me.

"Yes," I moaned, shuddering beneath the hungry caress of his tongue. He swirled it through me, reaching as deep into me as he could.

I didn't know his name. It didn't matter. This was a dream. A wonderful delight.

I clutched his hair and ground on his hungry mouth as he feasted on me. He sent such pleasure shuddering through me. My juices flowed into his mouth. He devoured me. His hands caressed my rump, pulling me tight against him. His tongue fluttered through me, stirring me up.

Such pleasure darted through me. Such a bliss to enjoy. I groaned, grinding against him, feeling his whiskers rasp on my shaved vulva. It was an incredible delight. My large tits heaved. I gasped as he found my clit, sucking on it. Nibbling on the sensitive bud.

It drove me wild. I let myself go, enjoying every moment of it. He sucked so hard, my bud aching between his lips. His tongue batted it, stroking it. Every caress made me quiver. My breasts swayed before me as the bliss swelled and swelled in my depths.

"I'm going to drown," I moaned, reveling in the passion swelling in me. "We're both going to drown!"

"Good," he growled. "Flood me with your passion. I want to drink your bounty, Goddess!"

Goddess...

I exploded. My pussy convulsed as he sucked on my clit again. I felt the juices gushing out of me, and a spicy musk filled my nose. It was so different from the sweet scent I was used to. It was a different sort of passion.

I gasped and groaned, my head tossing back and forth as he feasted on me.

He licked up the juices flooding out of me, sending new waves of delight washing through me. Bliss spilled through my body, splashing across my thoughts. I groaned, my eyes squeezing shut as I savored every bit of it. I loved the euphoria rushing through me. My mind drank it in, sparks bursting before my eyes.

It was incredible.

I lost all control of my body, clutching to his hair to keep from falling over. A dizzying euphoria swept through me. I couldn't keep my balance. I tottered backward, pulling away from him. I crashed onto a dark-maroon couch, my tits heaving as I trembled. I stared down at him through a universe of bursting stars. He licked his chops, face coated in my passion.

He peeled off his leather jacket as I squirmed, coming down from my orgasmic high. Then he tore off the t-shirt, revealing his sculpted physique. I moaned as he rose, towering over me. My eyes fell on his jeans. On that bulge.

He was so hung.

"I want you in me," I whimpered, delirious with passion. He'd given me so much when he ate me, but it wasn't enough.

I needed more.

"Look how you inspired me," he growled, ripping open his fly and shoving down his jeans. His cock sprang out, thrusting thick and long from a tangled mess of dark pubic hair. His balls swung heavy beneath his dick, full of his passion. He was so hard, so aching.

For me. Not for *her*. Me!

"Thank you," I moaned, reaching for him. I grasped his cock, feeling his girth throbbing in my grip. Those other women wanted him, but he brought this gift to me.

"I need to worship inside of you," he moaned as I pulled him towards me.

"Yes!" I panted, my thighs opened so wide. My pussy lips pulled apart, ready for him to enter me.

He leaned down, his lips claiming mine. He kissed me hard, thrusting his tongue into my mouth. I tasted my spicy juices on his mouth. A different flavor than I remembered.

I was someone else, but it was hard to hold onto that thought.

His body felt so right pressing on me. He was the one I wanted. Needed. I guided his cock between my thighs.

His tip nuzzled against my shaved folds, teasing me.

He thrust into me. A single plunge that buried him to the hilt in my depths. My cunt clenched around his girth while my thighs held him tight. My hands slid up his rippling abs, scratching at his barrel-deep chest. I whimpered into the kiss. His shaft reached deeper in me than any man had ever gone. He spread me so open.

He filled me.

I had never felt so full before. No man had ever taken my pussy to its limits. Never given me such passion and pleasure. I needed this. I whimpered and quivered, savoring him in me. I squeezed down on him, shifting my hips, ready for him to start pumping away in me.

I groaned into our kiss as he drew back his cock. My pussy clung to him, squeezing, not wanting to lose him. I felt so empty as he drew back more and more. I quivered when barely any of him was left in me.

He thrust back into me.

A wave of rapture washed through me, spawned by the surge of euphoria he churned in my pussy.

I kissed him with such hunger, my fingernails biting into his rock-hard muscles. My thighs clenched about him as he pumped his cock in and out of me. It was a slow rhythm, teasing. He made me quiver and I groaned, enjoying every moment. I could feel my passion growing, swelling.

He was where he belonged.

"Yes, yes, I'm almost there," I moaned as he drove that magnificent cock into the depths of my pussy again and again.

"Just surrender to my worship, Goddess," he growled, looming over me. His blue eyes penetrated my soul.

My fingernails scratched and clawed at his chest, raking burning furrows down his flesh. His dick slammed into me, filling my pussy to the hilt. His pubic bone ground into my clit. Sparks of wondrous delight burst from my nub and showered through me.

My orgasm erupted inside of me.

My pussy convulsed around his dick as he drew back. I writhed about him, celebrating the feel of him sliding through me. I groaned, my body trembling. My hips twitched, and my arms spasmed. The tattoo of the tiger on my inner forearm flashed before me as stars burst across my vision.

Pleasure surged through me as my pussy convulsed, clutching at his dick as he buried over and over in me. He grunted and growled, the beast in him unleashed by my climax. He slammed so hard into me, a bruising ache forming upon my labia.

It was incredible feeling the strength of his passion for me.

I heaved and gasped, bucking on the couch. My head arched, my neck rubbing against the cushion. My body twitched as the pleasure washed through me. His dick churned up my cumming pussy to a blissful froth, sending burst after burst of rapture through my body.

"Oh, my god, yes!" I squealed in delirious passion. "I feel your worship! Your fervor!"

He churned orgasm after orgasm through me. He gave me more pleasure than any man had ever delivered to me in my life. My thighs squeezed about his torso, gripping him as he plunged into my depths. My pussy sucked at his cock, aching to feel his seed spurting into me. I didn't care about protection. This was a dream; he could spill all his seed in me.

I never felt that before. I wanted him flooding me.

"Cum in me!" I howled. "Fill me with your love! Your worship!"

"My Goddess!" he growled.

His lips seized mine. He kissed me with such hunger, thrusting his tongue deep into my mouth as his cock buried into my convulsing snatch. His cum fired hot into me. Powerful blasts that splashed against my cervix. I reveled in his seed filling me. I groaned, savoring this wonderful treat flooding my snatch. I didn't know that it would feel this good.

It felt so right to have his cum spilling in me. I felt complete.

My orgasm melted my mind. The bliss intensified, my thoughts blurring into rapturous mush. Stars exploded across my vision. I gasped and convulsed, drowning as my pussy worked out every drop of cum he had in his heavy balls.

"I will remember you just like this, my Goddess!" he growled, all the passion burning in his voice.

"Yes!" I screamed and—

My eyes shot open. I was lying on my side, my pillow between my legs, my pussy soaking my panties. I groaned, quivering from the intense orgasm my dream-lover gave me. My entire body burned from the pleasure.

My round breasts rose and fell in my long nightshirt. I panted as I rolled onto my back, staring at the inner slope of my right forearm. There was no tattoo. I was awake, back in my body.

"Damn," I muttered to myself, my eyes fluttering. That dwarfed anything Tyrone ever gave me *before* he turned into an abusive asshole.

I felt so alive. Like I'd *truly* woken up from the dream of my life. I felt something amazing from the stranger. I never felt a dream that real before. It was like I had actually *become* that busty brunette. Part of me wondered if somewhere in the city she wasn't quivering on her couch right now, cumming on that hot hunk's big dick.

I moaned in wanton envy.

Then I noticed the cat watching me. She was perched on the foot of my bed, her green eyes staring at me. Her tongue flicked lazily across her chops. Then she hopped off and scampered out to my living room.

"Hope you enjoyed the show," I muttered. "Because *I* loved every minute of it."

Chapter Two: Memories of Him

Kyrie Hope

Ten minutes later, I was still keyed up from my orgasm. My orgasms. *Plural!*

It might've been a dream, but it was an amazing one. Though a languorous, euphoric haze had settled on me, I couldn't slide back into sleep. I was *energized* by the dream. I quivered, glancing at my smartphone resting on my nightstand.

I snagged it up, opening up Messenger. I found my friend, Cyndi, and sent her a quick message: *Just had the most amazing orgasm of my life. It was one hot sex dream.*

My breasts rose and fell, my nightshirt clinging to my round tits. I sat up and ripped off my sleepwear, freeing my familiar tits. My nipples were pink and hard, thrusting up at their normal size. I kinda missed being that busty brunette, but I had an amazing pair of breasts and a great body. I had nothing to be envious of. My mother always told me I should be happy with what I was given.

"Treasure what blessings the Lord has given you, Kyrie," she'd said a week before she fell asleep and didn't wake up again. She had that knowing smile on her lips when she spoke those words. The one that meant she was thinking about my father, Sterling. She had

a one night stand with the guy. Though my mom always said I was the best thing that came out of it, sometimes...

Sometimes she acted like their passion happened just last night, the memory fresh in her mind after all those years.

After this dream, I was starting to understand why it stayed with her for years and years, a memory she could sink into and remember being wholly a woman.

I bit my lip, glancing at the photo of my mother. The only personal item I took with me when I fled Tyrone. It was all I had left of her. She passed away shortly before I met Tyrone, claimed by a brain aneurysm.

Just as my thoughts were turning maudlin, the chime ring for my phone sounded, Cyndi answering me.

Oh, you have to give me the deets, she replied. She added a devilish emoji and a winky emoji to the end of her message.

Grinning, I texted, *I dreamed of that hunk who came into the bar tonight. You know, the one that had every gal melting.*

Cyndi answered with a splooshing water emoji, the universal sign of a woman getting wet.

Yep, that's the guy, I sent. *The weird part was, I dreamed I was another woman. That busty brunette with the tiger tattoo on her arm.*

That's weird, Cyndi answered. *What does it say about you that you dreamed you were someone else? Envious of her?*

Course I wasn't envious! I typed into the Messenger chat, fingers almost smashing my phone's screen.

Then why'd you dream you were her? Cyndi sent back along with another winky emoji.

I don't know why I was her, but it was amazing. He was such a stud!!! Knew how to make me cum!

Cyndi sent a laughing face emoji. *Sounds like it.* There was a pause then she added another line. *So who is this girl you dreamed you were? A busty brunette?*

The one with the tiger tattoo on her inner forearm. You pointed her out.

Oh, yes, I remember her. Those big tits almost spilling out of that cute, red dress she was wearing. I wish I had tits that big.

You have tits that big, I sent. *Yours are so perky for their size, too. Be proud of those tits.*

I think hers were bigger. They were gorgeous tits. Bet that stranger loved playing with them.

Well, her flirting must have worked because at least in my dreams, she had him tonight.

She wasn't the only one flirting, Cyndi typed with a winky emoji. *That stud was paying attention to you.*

My cheeks flushed as my thoughts drifted back to the club.

~~*~~

Earlier that evening...

"Damn, I can't take my eyes off of them," Cyndi said as she leaned towards me, her big, perky tits almost spilling out of the low-cut halter top she wore. The tattoo of the Ace of Spades on her right breast was half-exposed. She pushed the dainty, red-rimmed glasses she wore up her slender nose, her eyes flicking out at the stranger as he moved through the club.

Dance music pulsed and throbbed through the air. A lot of the women grinding on their partners were staring at him. There were guys scowling all over the place. None of them were happy about the rugged, darkly handsome stranger. He had that bad-boy look. Like James Dean. A rebel. Hungry. His sexy demeanor mixed with the physique of a powerful man, like a lumberjack or something. He looked dangerous and passionate. My body quivered every time his gaze swept over the bar.

"I know," I groaned to Cyndi. "I didn't think to bring a change of panties to work."

My friend gave an earthy giggle, her pillowy tits jiggling in her halter top. They were on the verge of spilling out and bouncing for all to see. Her short, blonde hair swayed about her face, her hazel eyes twinkling behind her glasses. "Tell me about it. My little thong is not keeping up. I'm glad I wore dark pants."

The stranger flicked his eyes over to us. His smile grew as I felt those piercing blues land on me. I quivered, shifting in my heeled boots as he sauntered towards me. I heard the leather jacket somehow rustling over the thudding music. He leaned on the bar, his roguish smile spreading across his thick lips. He had a shadow of stubble clinging to his sculpted jawline.

"What can I get you?" I asked brightly. I tried to keep the lust out of my voice. I wanted to be professional.

"A shot of Glenlivet," he said, his eyes flicking up and down me.

Cyndi quivered beside me; I could feel the envious waves coming off of her when he didn't even spare her a glance.

"Expensive taste," I said, turning around to grab the whiskey down from the top of the glowing, glass shelf. I snagged a tumbler and whirled back around, wanting to show off. I pulled out the glass stopper from the bottle and poured the amber drink with a smooth action. I slid it up to him, purring, "Bottoms up."

He winked at me, snagged it, and downed the expensive whiskey in a single swallow. He let out a deep groan of delight. "That is smooth. Ever tried it?"

I shook my head. "I'm more of an appletini girl."

"Why don't you pour yourself one and give it a try? Sometimes it's nice to live a little wild."

My pussy clenched as I snagged another shot glass. I pressed the two tumblers together and poured from one to the other, not spilling a drop. I hoisted the drink, watching the amber liquor slosh around, a tremble racing through me.

"To new meetings," he said, hunger in his voice.

I clinked my shot glass into his, then took a dainty sip while he threw his head back and drank his in a single swallow.

I almost coughed. It was strong, burning my tongue and the back of my throat. I gulped down my small mouthful and an instant warmth spread out of my stomach. It met the heat already melting my pussy. I quivered as he shook his head.

"Be wild and free," he said, leaning closer. His finger traced the back of my hand, sending fire racing down my nerve endings. My nipples hardened in a flash, my thighs squeezing together, putting pressure on my throbbing clit.

His blue eyes caught me. There was something about them, something at once both terrifying and arousing. They promised such passion, the pleasure that no woman would ever experience from another man. I raised the shot glass to my lips. I threw it back, the whiskey pouring over my tongue. I fought my splutters and swallowed.

I groaned, shuddering at the taste. It was smooth, but also had that strong flavor of distilled alcohol. That burning taste I preferred to blunt with fruity mixes. A shiver went through me, an almost orgasmic rush, as I set down my tumbler with a loud clink.

"Sometimes, it's fun to have adventures," he said, straightening. He pulled out two twenties, slipping them into my hand. He gave a nod of his head, almost like a cowboy from the Old West, before he turned and sauntered away.

The urge to abandon my post, to run out from behind the bar and chase him seized me. I felt like he wanted me to follow, but this was my job. I took it seriously. I needed the money.

My hands clenched on the two twenties as he reached the dance floor. Another woman snagged him up, black hair swaying about her face. Her green eyes flashed at me as she threw her arms around his neck, holding him tight. Her skin was a rich brown, giving her an exotic, bi-racial look. She melted against him, his hands grabbing her ass. They danced on the floor.

That could be me. A brunette in a red dress, the busty girl Cyndi had drooled over an hour ago, squirmed nearby, watching them dance just like I did.

"Damn," Cyndi moaned. "You're so lucky, Kyrie. He didn't even look at me."

I just swallowed, my throat burning from the whiskey, my

pussy a raging inferno of molten passion. "I wish my shift was over right now."

Cyndi nodded in agreement.

~~*~~

The present...

Oh, yes, there definitely were sparks between us, I typed to Cyndi. I hit send, my text bubble popping up on the Messenger app, my words outlined in blue.

Her response, surrounded by friendly yellow, answered, *Shame he left before we got off. Then you wouldn't have had to dream about him.*

Yeah, I answered. *Well, good night.*

Thanks for sharing. That was hoooooot!!! She added two more splooshing water emojis.

I smiled and set my phone on my breasts. I pondered why I was that other girl in my dreams. I sighed, rolled over onto my side, and closed my eyes.

He waited for me in my dreams. I sank into the safe embrace of his arms. I felt like he was watching me right now, protecting me from the world.

From Tyrone.

I slept peacefully until morning.

~~*~~

Dean Walker

I leaned against the corner of the building, the shadows around me. I stared up at the apartment across the street, seeing into its courtyard. The building's sign for the Coat of Arms Apartments illuminated the night.

I finally found her. She had to be the one. The moment I laid eyes on her tending bar, I knew. Something in my soul responded. She was important. A cog in the machinations of Hell. Some part of the schemes of one of the Seven Lords. I didn't know *how* she fit. I don't think she was even aware of what she was. It didn't matter.

Triumph surged through me.

My eyes fixed on her door, apartment 211. My thumb caressed over the tips of my fingers, the pads rough with calluses. My hungers quivered through me. She was such a beauty. I could feel the passion spilling off of her tonight. My soul desired to feast on her. Though I'd enjoyed another tonight, it was her I was thinking about.

I didn't know her name. Yet. But I would. I would awaken such passion in her. I would feast upon her and make her cry out in rapture.

A smile cracked my lips. I could just feel her thoughts quivering. They were full of memories of me. I breathed in, savoring that scent of lust seasoning the air. The sweet musk of her feminine passion.

"Finally," I whispered.

Chapter Three: Wanders Meet

Kyrie Hope

I woke up a few minutes before my alarm clock was set to go off. I felt amazing. I was still buzzing from the intensity of that dream about *him.* My eyes fluttered open, staring at the clock's digital numbers. They blazed red, the color of scarlet passion. I smiled, running my tongue over my lips while I quivered beneath my covers.

I had a few more minutes, so I dozed, holding onto that dream of the stranger for as long as possible. I may have been that busty brunette in it, but he still had loved *me.* No man had delivered such passion upon me. It was wonderful. Was this what my father had given my mother their one night together?

Maybe I would only get this one dream. I doubt I would ever see the stranger again. He didn't look like the type that stayed in one place. A wanderer. He must leave a trail of quivering women behind. All of them smiling. All of them remembering the one night they had him. It sustained them through the rest of their lives.

Through mediocrity.

I didn't want to settle for mediocrity. I wanted to have the best. I wanted him.

My eyes snapped open. I let out an angry hiss. "You better come back," I muttered to myself. "Because I want to—"

BEEP! BEEP! BEEP!

I slapped the button on top of my alarm clock, silencing the annoying chirp. I threw off my blanket, feeling invigorated for the day. Eager. Hopeful. Maybe he *would* show up tonight. I wanted to be ready if he did.

If the dream was that amazing, what would reality be like?

I was still just wearing my panties, my nightshirt discarded after the dream. My round breasts jiggled before me as I sauntered out of my bedroom. My door was open. That was unusual. I frowned, then remembered that stray cat that had entered my bedroom last night. How did she get in?

I must not have closed my bedroom door all the way in my exhaustion last night. She must've nudged it open enough to slip in.

After relieving my bladder, I headed through my small apartment to make myself my morning coffee. The cat was sleeping on my used couch. Her eyes flicked open just enough to glance at me before she closed them and resumed her ear-twitching dreams.

I shook my head, wondering where she came from. Such a striking cat. That glassy, black coat and those vibrant, green eyes. I noticed she had no collar as I waited for my coffee to percolate. I frowned, wondering if I had anything to feed her.

I opened my refrigerator and noticed some chicken that was about to spoil. I bought it on sale, but it was more than I could eat before it passed the use by date. I found a little bowl and dropped the meat in there.

The cat appeared like a flashing shadow, purring, rubbing against my naked calf before descending on the feast. I sipped my coffee and smiled. It was nice having someone to share the apartment with. Her tail swished back and forth, twitching.

I came more more awake, my body buzzing with delight. My shift at the club started soon. I had to get ready.

"I guess you're staying with me, huh?" I asked. "Us strays have to stay together, right?"

She lifted her head and gave me this flat look as if saying, *"I am no stray. But I'll take care of you anyways."*

I giggled. There was something... reassuring about the arrogance of a cat. It was something you could count on. They were reliable in their own way. I knelt down and stroked her back, loving the warmth of her. The way she purred. Her happiness rumbled through her skin, caressing me. I wanted to keep petting her, but work awaited.

He awaited.

Humming, the human form of purring, I sauntered to my bathroom. I stepped out of my panties, hopped into the shower, and groaned in delight as the warm water splashed over me. Ten minutes later, I felt warm and scrubbed clean. I undid my hair, not wanting to get it wet, and set about applying my makeup.

I always took care with my makeup, making sure everything was applied right, but today, I was extra careful. The right shade of ruby lipstick. The appropriate eye shadow to make my baby blues sparkle. Just a touch of rouge to highlight my delicate cheekbones. I took care to make my good features stand out. I appeared both beautiful, but also wholesome. That girl-next-door sort of look. Maybe it wasn't what the guy was into, but he had come up and flirted with me.

Me!

Not my friend Cyndi.

Another giddy thrill ran through me at that thought.

Humming louder, I attacked my fiery hair with my brush. I combed it out until it fell in a lustrous sheen of brassy-red hair. It always cooperated. I never had a bad hair day. My natural curls always fell about my face, enhancing my beauty.

I nodded when I was done, my green eyes twinkling in the mirror. I looked naughty but not whorish; beautiful not slutty. I was looking to have fun, to be flirty, to attract his attention.

I was almost late to work because I couldn't settle on an outfit.

I tore through my closet, wanting to find the perfect look. The panties were easy, a thong slipping between my butt-cheeks and nestling against my pussy. A few red hairs of my trimmed bush peeked out, but that seemed to enhance the naughtiness of wearing them. After searching my closet, I finally settled upon a deep-red halter top. It lifted my breasts into a pair of delicious mounds; a nice amount of cleavage to entice the eyes. The black, spaghetti straps left my shoulders mostly bare. It fitted like a corset, so I didn't need to wear a bra with it, the top giving my tits more than enough support. It also left a few inches of my midriff bare, showing off my cute bellybutton.

Then came the toughest decision: skirt or pants.

I didn't know if I wanted tight jeans or a sexy skirt. Both had their advantages. Normally, I wore jeans or other pants to work, but I wanted to be adventurous tonight. I wanted to signal that I was here to have fun. I grabbed a short, pleated, black skirt. It hugged my waist and fell down my rump and thighs. The slightest movement made it swish and swirl, drawing eyes to my gorgeous legs. My heeled boots, reaching up to just below my knees, finished the outfit.

"I'm going to melt his heart if he shows up," I said to myself as I strutted out of my bedroom. "What do you think, Shadow?"

The cat lifted her head off the couch, opening her green eyes. She seemed to give a slight nod, like she approved.

"You don't mind if I call you Shadow, right?" I asked. I didn't feel foolish at all for talking to the cat. She was so intelligent.

She gave a lazy flick of her ears then rested her head back on her paws, her eyes closing shut. She didn't seem like she cared at all.

"Well, Shadow, don't destroy my apartment. I'll pick you up some proper food on my way home."

Her tail flicked idly.

I hoped the twenty-four-hour convenience store near my apartment sold cat food. I was pretty sure it did.

I rushed into the bar at the last minute before my shift started. I blinked, surprised by how many women were already here. It was early for The Green Eye Delight to become crowded. It was even weirder for there to be this many women.

What was going...?

Oh, right. I had competition.

Groaning, I darted to the back room and dropped off my purse. I pulled on my black half-apron, then returned to tend bar. Cyndi was already there, helping to get things ready.

"Look at all the skanks waiting for *him* to show up," she said, shaking her head. Her blonde hair danced about her face, her red-rimmed glasses shifting on her nose. "They're all asking if your dream-lover has shown up."

"Has he?" I asked, peering around.

Cyndi giggled. "No, he hasn't. I see they're not the only one who dressed up tonight."

My cheeks burned even as I said, "Can you blame me? It was the best sex I ever had, and it was only a dream. I can only imagine what it would be like to be with him in real life."

Cyndi nodded her head, such envy in her hazel eyes.

"Well, I see you also dressed up for him," I told Cyndi.

She giggled, her large tits almost spilling out of the tight, leather top she wore. It hugged her almost like a corset or a tube top. It lifted her breasts into jiggling mounds. Her slightest breath caused them to quiver. Even more of her Ace of Spades tattoo peeked out tonight, and I could even see a hint of her pink areolas. Her black pants were so tight, I don't know how she got them on short of being poured into them. It was clear she wasn't wearing panties. Guys were going to enjoy seeing her cameltoe tonight.

For the next few hours I worked while a growing group of disconsolate guys slumped to the bar, faces long. They were all striking out on the women while more and more ladies showed up. They gathered in small cliques and groups. All gossiping with each other and staring daggers at those they didn't like. It was like a dozen prides of lionesses stalked the club, all waiting for their prey to arrive.

Only this prey would devour them.

I giggled when I thought that.

The music was pounding through the club, but the tips weren't flowing. Guys were more generous than girls, especially when they were having a good time. Sadly, none of them were having one. Despite the DJ's beats, hardly anyone was dancing. The girls were all quivering, waiting for *him* to arrive.

Then, despite the pounding beat of trance music, a hush fell over the club. My nipples instantly went hard. My pussy molten. I groaned, my head snapping towards the club's entrance. There he was, sauntering in, wearing that dark, leather jacket. He wore a red t-shirt tonight, the fabric molding to his pecs. His jeans were dark, fitting tight. The women all quivered and moaned together. Then they descended upon him, a flock of beautiful vultures all wanting to feast.

I was stuck behind the bar.

He moved through them, striding with a hungry grace. His hands were everywhere, groping asses, stroking cheeks, even squeezing breasts through low-cut tops. Women quivered and moaned, his very touch almost sending them into orgasmic spasms. It was like he was lust incarnate. Masculine perfection thrust into the world.

It seemed impossible, yet there he was.

My pussy only grew wetter and wetter, my poor thong soaked in a second. My bush couldn't constrain the flood. I felt lines of juices trickling down my inner thighs. Cyndi groaned beside me, quivering as he swept through the bar.

"Oh, god, he's coming towards you," said Cyndi, her silver nose ring flashing.

My back straightened as I realized his blue eyes kept falling on me as he moved through the women. I quivered, and the entire club grew dark save for this illumination around him. I knew it was all my head, but it was like the world shone a spotlight on him just for me. He came closer and closer, that hungry grin growing on his face.

He broke free of a horde of women and reached the bar, leaning his hands on the darkly polished surface. "There is the adventurous barmaid," he said, his voice a rumbling bass caressing my body. "What fun are you having tonight?"

I shuddered, my heart thudding in my chest. I needed to say something. With more confidence than I felt, I leaned over and, letting him stare down my bodice at my tits, purred, "I don't know. You want to buy more of that expensive whiskey, or are you in the mood for something... different?"

"Why don't you choose what sort of fun we have," he said, his hand moving just enough to brush the back of my own, his fingers rough and strong like they were in the dream.

A shiver of heat flowed down my arm and reached throughout my body. My nipples both tingled as the wave washed down my torso towards my molten sex. I couldn't help the whimpering moan that burst from my lips. My cheeks burned at the girlish sound I made.

I straightened, wanting to appear mature. After all I was twenty-four. So I said in a cool tone, "I think I have just the thing."

I whirled around, my pleated skirt swirling about my thighs. I felt his gaze on my rump as I sauntered to the glass shelf, illuminated with a soft blue light, that held our liquor. This exhilaration ran through me. This was such a new game, something I hadn't done in such a long time. Since I was that vulnerable girl, the death of my mother still fresh.

Not since I wandered into the arms of that predator.

"Now, people think this is the best whiskey we have," I said, pulling down a bottle of Macallan. "Everyone seems to think it's even better than the Glenlivet."

He nodded his head, saying, "It's a good whiskey. I prefer Glenlivet."

"But Macallan is also the boring go-to one," I said. "The real fun is found with this one." I shifted a few steps to my right to grab another bottle. "Now this is a whiskey that a man like you will appreciate. A thirty-year-old Highland Park. It's expensive, but..."

He arched an eyebrow, seeing the label. He nodded his head approvingly. I shuddered, glad I'd pleased him with my choice. I may not like drinking whiskey, but I knew every single drink in the bar and what people thought about them. I had to so I could make recommendations to my customers.

I believed a job should be done right.

I sauntered back to him on my booted heels, my hips swaying. I was so aware of the jiggle of my braless tits in my halter top. I snagged two tumblers and set them on the darkly polished bar. Just like last time, I poured back and forth between each of them, not spilling a drop while filling them to the brim. He grinned at me, sliding one closer to my hand.

I snagged it.

"I don't even know your name," I said, giving him a grin as I raised my glass for a toast. "It's kinda... exciting."

He nodded his head. We clinked our drinks together. This time, I tossed it back in a single gulp like he did. A shudder ran through my body. The Highland Park was as strong as the Glenlivet, and still burned my throat. My right leg twitched, the heel of my boot thudding on the ground as I shivered through swallowing it. That warmth drifted down my gullet to my stomach. It spread out, buzzing through my body, enhancing the heat already blazing in my pussy.

"Better," he said, grinning at me. "You didn't cough this time."

"Well, you're just inspiring," I said, winking at him.

He chuckled. "Another?"

"Are you trying to get me drunk?" I asked, arching an eyebrow. "I didn't think you had to stoop to that level."

He laughed, a deep, rumbling bass. "Never hurts. But what are you saying, though? That I could snap my fingers, and you'd come running?"

I shuddered, a strange part of me wanting him to snap his digits. "Do I look that easy?"

His eyes slid over to where Cyndi was working at the other end of the bar. "Definitely not as easy as some."

"Or that desperate fan club around you?" I was so aware of the women building behind him, all glaring at me.

"Jealous?"

"Why?" I leaned closer to him, my red hair swaying about my

cheeks, and purred, "You're talking to me, aren't you?"

His grin grew. "You're just so intriguing."

I winked at him and poured a second round of drinks. I picked up my shot glass. Before we clinked them together, he asked, "What is your name, barmaid?"

"Kyrie," I said. "Kyrie Hope."

"Kyrie," he said, his deep voice caressing my name like his hands had danced across my body in the dream. A shudder ran through me. "I'm Dean. Dean Walker."

"Oh, yeah? Got the name of a wanderer, don't you?" I said. "Just leaving a string of broken hearts in your wake?"

"I leave behind a string of satisfied women," he said, winking at me.

I bet that busty brunette was at home still quivering in delight from the night she had with him. I almost asked about her, but why talk about another woman?

"To a pair of wanderers meeting," I said, lifting my shot glass in the air.

We clinked them together.

It went down smoother this time. I didn't shudder as much, and it tasted better, my body growing warmer from the buzz. I flexed my fingers let out a purring moan of delight. "I'm starting to see the appeal of whiskey. There is a boldness to it. Just sort of seizes you. Imposes its passion upon you. I felt like I was submitting to it."

He grinned at me then asked, "A wanderer, too, huh? How did you end up tending bar then?"

I hesitated. "Well, wanderer isn't *quite* the right term for me. Just... struggling to find a new place in this world after my life ended."

He nodded his head. "We all have the past we're dragging behind us, chains pulling upon our souls."

"Yeah," I said, hating the dour turn of the conversation.

His blue eyes brightened. "So why be a barmaid?"

"I like bars. They're dark places. It's fun to watch people and see how they act. How they pretend to be something they're not.

Some are good at it, adopting a confidence and their bravado. Men and women both. They all come here searching for something. Sometimes, they even find it."

"Sometimes," he said. He shifted his tumbler around on the bar's polished surface. "You just like to watch, huh? A bit of a voyeur?"

A hot shudder ran through me. I almost was like a voyeur in that dream, the ultimate one. I inhabited the brunette's body. I witnessed her delight through her own eyes, experiencing her pleasure with this man vicariously.

I shivered and said, "Maybe I am, Dean."

"So you never want to get out there and... act?" he asked, straightening.

I swallowed, a quick flutter of fear from the last time I acted shooting through me. I favored him a smile, saying, "It doesn't pay the bills."

"Nothing can tempt you?"

I swallowed, a hot tremble rippling through me. "Well..."

He leaned closer. "Well, what does it take?" he asked. His fingers brushed my hand again. "Huh, Kyrie?"

"Well, maybe with the right guy," I said, my voice tight. His finger traced a pattern on the back of my hand, sending such a wicked sensation through my body.

His grin grew as he straightened. He pulled out another pair of twenties, pressing them into my palm. "Thank you for the drinks. They were... invigorating."

My hand clenched down on the bills as he turned around. He swaggered away from me, leaving me quivering. He glanced once over his shoulder at me, his gaze meeting mine. He had such a roguish quality to him, teasing me. I could feel it even as he scooped up a blonde in a skimpy, blue dress, the thin triangles of cloth barely covering her small breasts.

She melted to his side while the other girls all groaned in disappointment. She clung to him as he led her out onto the dance floor, his hand sliding down from her waist to grip her ass. I was surprised I wasn't jealous. I wanted this guy bad, and there he was with another girl.

But it was almost like he was... enticing me to come out and play. To abandon my little hiding place behind the bar and have fun.

However, I was working. I had customers to help. I couldn't just abandon my responsibilities to dance with the hottest guy in the world. My poor thong was a sodden mess while I squeezed my thighs together.

I couldn't look away as the blonde's arm slipped around his neck. He had both his hands on her ass now, pulling her tight against him. Despite the fast song, they were grinding together; a slow dance.

"Oh, my god, that dress," Cyndi moaned in envious delight. "Did you see how it barely covers her tits?" She glanced down at her own ample bosom. "I'd look amazing in that dress."

"I would look more amazing pressed against him," I muttered.

"Definitely," Cyndi moaned. "In that dress. Mmm, I'd just eat that blonde out. I could just devour her. Devour them both."

I nodded my head in partial agreement. The guy, definitely. Then a customer sidled up, forcing my attention away from Dean.

Damn, why did I have to be so responsible?

~~*~~

Dean Walker

My finger remembered the feel of the back of Kyrie's hand.

The blonde in the blue dress whimpered as she ground against me, the music pulsing around us. I let my lust bleed into her, teasing her. Already, as an orgasm built in her nethers, my hungers ached to feed on her. The devil half of me begged to devour her, reveling in the passion bleeding out of her soul. It was a feast she offered.

This club was a buffet for a cambion of my descent. A feast for an incubus to enjoy. So many women desiring me. I nibbled on all their lusts, gaining strength from their passion for me. My dick was so hard as the blonde ground against me. Her ass flexed beneath my fingers through the thin fabric of her dress.

My fingers remembered Kyrie...

I gripped the blonde's rump, groped her. I pulled her tight against my throbbing dick as my gaze once again slipped towards Kyrie. She was helping another customer, not looking at me.

This other man held her attention.

Despite that, I could feel her passion beating over the other women in the club. There was a darkness inside of Kyrie. In her blood. She didn't know it, was unaware of her heritage, but it called to me as much as her ardor. She had to be like me. She was special, the reason I had come here. Whatever the Dukes of Hell wanted with her, I would thwart it.

I would ruin their plans.

My anger flashed into passion.

"Yes," the blonde whimpered, quivering against me as her orgasm burst through her. "Yes, yes, you're such a stud!"

I could smell her tart musk perfuming the air, her passion soaking through her panties. I devoured her lust spilling through her body, her soul. My incubus-half devoured every bit of her climax's energy. It fed me, strengthened me. The women in the bar all quivered. Even Kyrie shuddered, her gaze darting towards me. She straightened, such pride rippling through her as she went back to pouring a drink, trying to fight the lust surging through the room.

I couldn't get her out of my head. Those green eyes, her red hair. She was playful. Flirty, but not too aggressive. She wanted to have fun, but she had self-control. She was a good girl who wanted to be wild. Passionate. She reminded me so much of Terra.

Thinking Terra's name hurt.

I gripped the blonde's ass, holding her tight to me as she quivered through her orgasm. Then she stumbled away from me, fanning her face while another wanton woman darted towards me, eager to dance. Eager to feed my devilish hungers.

But I wanted to feast on Kyrie tonight.

40

~~~*~~~

Kyrie Hope

Woman after woman danced with Dean. All left him shuddering, the lust shining on their faces. They all trembled like they'd cum. All he did was grind on them, groping their tits or asses through their dresses. He would whisper in their ears or maybe nibble on their necks, but that was it.

However, every one of them had such a huge smile when they finished.

Dancing with him appeared to be the next best thing to sex. I quivered, wanting to be with him so bad, aching to just abandon the bar and dart out there. To be wild. Naughty. To let my lust flow for once.

Instead, I took out the trash.

Another girl had shown up to work the club. Barley was a cutie with brown hair. Her arrival let me have a quick breather, a chance to gather myself. I snagged the trash bags from beneath the bar, wanting to enjoy my break in the alley out back after dropping them off at the dumpster. I fanned my face with my free hand as I carried out the garbage. I groaned when I burst out into the cooler night air. I needed this break.

From him.

I dropped the trash bags into the dumpster and let the lid slam down with a clang. I turned around, my thoughts still full of him, when I smelled something. That leather musk. I shuddered at the familiarity of that scent. A quiver ran through me, a heat bursting in my loins. The shadows in the alley suddenly felt so intense, so deep and dark.

Almost as if he bled out of them, Dean appeared.

He stepped into the light shining from above the door that led back into the club; his blue eyes almost glowed. They appeared incandescent as they flicked up and down my body. My nipples hardened in a flash. A hot shiver ran through me. I couldn't believe he was here. His presence pulled at my nethers, magnetic and intense.

I couldn't think. I just acted.

Chapter Four: Good Girl Going Wild

Kyrie Hope

I couldn't stop myself from crossing to him. The lust that had been brewing in my body since the dream overwhelmed me. This man was something different. Something I'd never encountered in my life. I wanted to enjoy him in reality. To be wild this one time, and experience what I'd only dreamed about. I remembered how I came awake feeling reborn.

I flowed to him in a flash.

My arms were around his neck, my body pressed tight against him. He was just a solid as he was in the dream, just as physically present. I felt his warmth bleeding through our clothing, felt the ardor he had for me. My lips met his, kissing him like I had in the dream.

Only this time it was *my* lips that tasted him, not that brunette's.

His arms swept around me, pulling me tight. He groaned into the kiss, his lips working, teasing mine. I quivered as we shared this moment, the both of us feasting on the other. His hand stroked my back, caressing me through my halter top. My nipples throbbed as they felt the strength of his chest.

I rubbed myself against him, wiggling, feeling every bit of him I could. Especially that hard bulge. He was as impressive as he was in the dream. How had I conjured him so perfectly? How had I dreamed up something so similar to the reality of him?

His right hand drifted down, caressing the exposed strip of skin of my lower back. He traced the groove of my spine, sending shivers that raced through my body, ending at my nipples and pussy. My cunt clenched as I whimpered into the kiss, my tongue playing with his.

His finger brushed the waistband of my skirt. Then he was stroking down it, following the line of my butt-crack. He pressed my skirt into the divide between my asscheeks, molding the satin cloth to my rump. I shuddered as he squeezed my asscheek, kneading me as he pulled me tight against his girth.

He throbbed with his passion for me.

This almost terrifying chill swept through me. I was kissing a man I barely knew. I was letting myself be wild. This was crazy, exciting, and scary. Where were would these emotions take me? Was I really going to let him take me here?

Behind the club?

He broke the kiss, his right hand squeezing my ass in an almost comforting way. "Kyrie, I'm only going to take you where you want to go."

I shuddered against him.

"I'm only going to give you what you crave. What you need. You don't have to be afraid. I'm not going to hurt you." His blue eyes swallowed my universe, the endless depths of a warm ocean. "I'm just giving you the pleasure that you ache for.

"That you deserve."

I shuddered at his words and moaned, "Yes!"

I kissed him again, thrusting my tongue into his mouth. It was time for me to play. I could enjoy myself. He held me tight, gripping me as he turned us. He pressed me back until I felt the rough bricks of the club's exterior rasping against my bare shoulders. He pinned me there, kissing me with such hunger. I felt so helpless and yet...

Safe.

Dean wouldn't hurt me. He just wanted to love me.

I could feel that about him. He was passionate about women. That was why he danced with them one after the other, giving each one a chance to experience a taste of his passion. To leave him, quivering and gasping and shuddering. Through it all, he wanted one woman above the rest.

He wanted me.

I kissed him with a passion I'd never given another man, not even Tyrone. I held nothing back, my left arm hooked about his neck, holding his lips to mine while my right scratched down his back, clawing at his leather jacket. I breathed in the smell of him, that musk of manly passion. I trembled, writhing and undulating my hips, grinding against his bulge. Dry-humping against him. I needed him so bad. The dream was just a preview of this moment.

He broke the kiss, his blue eyes burning. "What do you want? Show me the desires coursing through you. Let me feel what I can give *you.*"

I shuddered and gasped, "You only give? Do women never do things for you?"

"Giving them what they crave gives me what I desire," he said, his dick throbbing against me. "It feeds my soul."

This strange desire seized me. Tyrone would always make me suck him. He always wanted me to go down on his cock, loving seeing me on my knees. Even if he was going to fuck me, he'd want me to start out that way. I hated it. He never would go down on me unless I begged. And later on, I realized that pleading was always a mistake.

Now, with Dean, I had a chance for a fresh beginning. I was reborn.

I would do something for this man that other women didn't. I could feel it. They were greedy. Always taking from him.

"You sure, Kyrie?" he asked like he knew what I was thinking. Like he could read my passion.

"Yes, let me give you something," I moaned. After last night, after the passion of my dream, I wanted to please him. Even if he didn't know how much pleasure he'd already given me, I wanted to make him happy.

Then I knew he would make me explode.

"Well, I never say no to a woman," he said, a grin sliding across his lips as he stepped back.

I sank to my knees with determination. The wild passion consumed me. I was going to claim my sexuality. I was going to love Dean Walker in ways I never would willingly do for that bastard.

My hands shot to the fly of his jeans. He had a belt on that I hadn't noticed, black and thick, closed by a silver buckle. I worked it, prying at the stiff leather. I was eager to get at the bulge tenting the front of his jeans. My pussy clenched, the heat building and building inside of me. My tongue flicked across my lips.

I was so eager to suck him. To blow this guy.

"You should never feel ashamed of your desires, Kyrie," he said, rumbling comfort found in his voice. "Express yourself. Show me your passions."

"Yes," I growled as I undid his belt. The two ends hung loose as I attacked the fastener of his jeans. "I'm gonna love you with my mouth. I'm gonna show you such bliss. Thank you."

His head cocked to the side, smile intense. "You are a rare woman, Kyrie Hope."

I winked at him.

His jeans came undone and his zipper rasped as I wrenched his fly open. His cock tented the plaid boxers he wore beneath. I hooked my fingers in their waistband and tugged them down. His jeans fell off his hips and down to his knees, belt rustling. I licked my lips at his exposed, muscular thighs. They were just as thick and powerful as they were in my dreams. The tip of his cock caught on his boxers' elastic waistband. I yanked down hard.

He sprang out before me.

My pussy ached at the memory of this shaft pounding me in my dreams. My mouth salivated as I stared at it up close. I never thought of a cock as gorgeous before, but the shaft... It was beautiful. Long and hard, ending at a swollen, pink crown. Clear precum bubbled from the tip, the salty scent filling my nostrils when I inhaled.

I grabbed his cock in a firm grip, not afraid. I stroked up and down him, feeling the hard flesh beneath the softer skin. More precum bubbled from his slit as I fisted him, my hand milking the lubrication out of him.

A hunger seized me. My head darted forward, my tongue flicking out. He groaned as my tongue licked up his crown and flicked across his slit. I gathered his precum on my tongue, shuddering as the salty flavor melted across my taste buds.

I purred my delight, waves of heat washing out of my pussy. My left hand found his heavy balls, kneading them as I nuzzled my lips against the tip of his cock. I sucked half his crown into my mouth, lips sealed tight. He groaned as I fisted him and fondled his heavy nuts. I loved him, feeling so wild and wanton. I was enjoying what all those women on the dance floor ached for.

More more of my lips slipped over his cock. I engulfed all of his crown, feeling every bit of the mushroom-shaped helmet sliding into my mouth. My tongue swirled and danced around it, making him groan and gasp. Pleasure twisted across his face. I gave him this delight.

I was happy to satiate him.

I stroked my hand up and down his dick, fisting him as I sucked and loved him. My head twisted, pressing his cock against my left inner cheek and then my right. I rubbed him up against the roof of my mouth, stimulating him. I wanted to give him as much bliss as possible.

"Goddamn, Kyrie," he growled, his voice thick with his passion. "I knew you were adventurous. Out of all those women in the club, you're the one who *truly* wanted to live. Wanted to get wild."

I sucked harder, drinking in his words. His moans. I put the same enthusiasm into blowing his cock that he put into licking my pussy during the dream. He'd worshiped my cunt, so I worshiped his dick. I sucked hard as my head bobbed, fucking my mouth up and down his shaft.

I didn't feel demeaned as the saliva dribbled down my chin. I didn't feel like he was using me as I sucked with all my might. I craved his salty seed spilling across my tongue. I wanted to taste him. To make him cum. I kneaded his nuts, feeling them heavy with his passion. I sucked even harder, my cheeks hollowing.

"Fuck, you're good," he moaned, pleasure twisting his face. His right hand seized my red hair, gripping me.

Not even that made me feel demeaned. Instead, it made me feel like a woman. I was inspiring this much passion in him. This felt so right.

"That's it," he moaned. "You're going to get what you crave. Keeps sucking like that, Kyrie. I'm going to drown you with my cum."

A flutter rippled out of my clenching cunt. My clit throbbed against my sodden thong. My thighs pressed together as I wiggled my hips. I wanted that. I moaned with all my passion, sucking so hard as I bobbed my head faster. His balls tightened in my hand. I could feel it coming, that eruption.

I craved it. I ached for it.

My tongue swirled and fluttered around the shaft. I formed such a powerful suction as I slid my lips up his shaft before I slammed my lips back down his cock, his tip brushing the back of my throat. I rubbed his spongy crown across the roof of my mouth, loving how he groaned. More and more of his precum filled my mouth.

That salty preview of the true delight to come.

"Kyrie," he growled. "Fucking shadows of Hell," he growled. "By all of Gehenna's pleasures and punishments, yes!"

His hot cum spurted into my mouth. I groaned and quivered, a little orgasm sweeping through me as the flavor burst to life on my taste buds. I gulped down his seed, my pussy convulsing. More juices soaked my poor thong, unable to contain the tide of my passion. It was so sexy making him cum. It turned me on so much to swallow his seed.

It warmed down to my belly. It fed the fire burning in my pussy. I squirmed as he kept erupting. He fired far, far more jizz than Tyrone ever did. Dean didn't taste too bitter, either, but just the right amount of salty bliss. I guzzled down his cum.

I swallowed every drop, sucking hard, savoring every bit of it.

"Kyrie," he groaned, "thank you. Thank you for trusting me. Thank you for that bliss. Goddamn, you're amazing. I have to fuck you. I have to make you cum even harder. I need to feel that pussy spasming on my snatch."

I popped my mouth off his dick, nodding as I groaned, "Please, please, pound me."

"I want to take you to the heights of rapture. I went to lift you from the drudgery of Hell into the light of Paradise."

His words swept through me. I quivered as he seized my elbows and lifted me to my feet. I shuddered, the flavor of his salty cum lingering on my lips. He pressed me back against the wall, his hands tearing up my skirt. He exposed my thong, the skimpy, black garment soaked with my juices. His fingers hooked the narrow band, ripping it to the side so his cock could ram into me.

"Yes, yes, fuck me, Dean!" I howled, my voice echoing through the alley. "Take me to Paradise."

Dean's dick speared into my pussy.

His girth sank into me in a single plunge, burying into my liquid depths. I groaned, quivering against the brick wall of the club. He was just as large in reality as he was in my dream, stretching and stretching my pussy to its limits. A wave of pleasure rippled through my body, tracing through all my nerve endings.

It reached my mind, splashing rapture across my thoughts. Little stars twinkled through the darkness of the alley as he nuzzled into my neck.

Dean growled as he drew back his hips, his dick sliding through my juicy depths. I clenched about him, shuddering as I savored him. I wanted him to thrust back into me, to bury to the hilt in me and make me explode.

He slammed back into me, his cock filling my pussy's depths. I groaned and quivered, my snatch squeezing around him. Every thrust of his cock into my snatch sent new waves of delight flooding through me. I loved it.

"Oh, Dean, yes!" I howled, my passion echoing down the alley. My arms wrapped about his neck, his leather jacket rubbing against my forearms. "This cock is just as good as I remembered!"

"Remembered?" he growled, his hips driving forward with such passion. He was that beast unleashed.

"In my dreams!" I howled, my eyes flicking around, not focusing on anything as my body trembled beneath the pleasure of his thrust.

He growled out in pure delight. His whiskered cheek rubbed against my sensitive neck as his hot lips kissed upward. He reached my jawline, then his tongue licked up to my ear. I groaned as he nibbled on it while driving his dick in and out of my juicy cunt. He churned me towards that amazing pleasure as he teased my earlobe, his tongue playing with my earring.

"Your thoughts are just full of me, huh?" he growled. "Wishing I visited you like an incubus in the night."

"Yes!" I gasped, my pussy clenching down so hard on his dick. Was that what had happened? "Oh, God, it was the best sex of my life and it was only a dream."

"So what's this?" he growled, his dick slamming into my cunt. His pubic bone smacked my clit, my little bud throbbing in delight.

"This is reality!" I moaned, my nipples aching as they rubbed against his chest through our clothing. "This is even better! You're in me, Dean!"

With a hungry growl, he claimed my lips. He kissed me, pinning my body so tight against the wall. I squirmed my hips, undulating and meeting the powerful rhythms of his thrust. I clung to him, kissing him with such passion as he brought me closer and closer to my rapture.

I could feel that growing orgasm, a sweet explosion promising to consume me in ecstasy. His every thrust fed my blossoming rapture. It swelled the pressure in the depths of my womanhood. At the very core of my femininity.

Feeling bold, I threw my thighs around his waist, his strength pinning me against the wall. He held me up, his hand seizing my ass. His fingers dug like iron into my rump as he drove that amazing dick in and out of me.

It was so big. I couldn't take much more of this.

I broke the kiss and screamed out, "Wanderer!"

"Let yourself explode," he growled. "Gehenna's fires, just let it burst out of you."

His cock buried to the hilt in me. His pubic bone ground against my clit. The sparks exploded rapture through me. My pussy convulsed.

My orgasm detonated in my depths.

Sweeping pleasure washed out of my convulsing cunt. My snatch writhed and spasmed around his dick. My pussy celebrated this pleasure. Every joyous thrust of his cock spread the rapture. This amazing man gave me bliss. My eyes fluttered as waves of darkness washed across my vision, bringing with them a starry expanse of ecstasy.

I kissed him hard as the winds of passion whipped rapture through my body. My thighs clenched around his waist, his leather jacket rustling as he pumped his cock in and out of my writhing depths. He kept my pleasure going; spilled my orgasms from one to the other.

I couldn't tell where one climax began and another ended. I was awash in pleasure, moaning into his kiss. My fingers stroked his whiskered cheeks as our tongues dueled with ferocity. My pussy sucked at him, hungry for his jizz. I wanted his cum spilling into me. I wanted to feel his seed spurting into my hungry depths.

My pussy convulsed with writhing ecstasy. My flesh massaged him, sucking at his girth. My cunt loved his dick. I squirmed against the wall, my fingernails scratching at his face, my other hand gripping the leather of his jacket.

I broke the kiss and howled, "Cum in me! Give me your

passion! I want it. I want to feel like a woman. *Your* woman!"

"Kyrie, right now you're all mine!" he snarled and drove his cock into the depths of my pussy.

I felt the first hot spurts of his jizz firing into me. The salty passion pumped from his cock into my spasming depths. My pussy writhed about his girth, milking him. I wanted more and more of his worship to fill me. I shuddered against him, my eyes blinking as wanton darkness washed across my vision.

A new orgasm exploded through me.

Rapture welled through my flesh. It filled every inch of me. My body bucked and convulsed against him, my nipples throbbing through my halter top as they rubbed against his muscular chest. I whimpered as more and more of his seed pumped into me. He filled me with his passion. I never wanted this to stop.

"My goddess," he growled. "My devilish muse. Feel my rapture? Feel what you inspired in me?"

"Yes!" I howled, my voice echoing down the alley. "I feel it, Dean!"

We kissed again, his tongue dueling with mine as my orgasm peeked. Pleasure reached our shared heights, a plateau of ecstasy I never wanted to leave. I clung to the bliss—clung to *him*—as the ecstasy rippled through me.

Then it died.

My legs lowered to the ground. Our kiss became sweet, verging on loving. His lips were so strong against mine, so demanding. His tongue caressed me, loving me. I trembled in delight, coming down from this heady moment.

"Dean, thank you," I moaned. "I needed that."

"We both did, my devilish muse," he said before he pulled his cock out of me. He still felt hard. Like he hadn't gone soft.

I frowned, realizing he'd cum in my mouth and then fucked my pussy without needing any recovery. This man had passion.

"You're going back to them?" I asked, my breasts rising and falling.

"Do you want me to stay?" he replied, his blue eyes piercing.

I almost said yes. Part of me wanted to beg for that, but I didn't know him. We just shared an amazing passion between two wanderers who met this one night and would never see each other again. "I have to go back to my work," I panted. "Tend bar."

He stroked my cheek, sending a fiery shiver down my spine. "You'll always be my devilish muse, Kyrie. If you want me, you'll find me."

And then he almost vanished into the shadows as he strolled away, like the darkness hugged him, his lover embracing him. I panted, struggling to catch my breath, reeling, his cum soaking into my thong. My panties had slid back into place, trapping his lust inside of me. I quivered there until Cyndi found me, looking concerned until she saw the passion in my eyes.

"Someone got lucky," she said with that envious smile on her lips.

"Yeah," I panted. "My one lucky night with him." I felt good about that. My break was over. Time to get back to work.

Chapter Five: Dreams of Shadow

Kyrie Hope

Cyndi took my hand and pulled me from the wall. I pushed down my pleated skirt while stumbling after her still half-dazed by the power of my orgasms. Dean had given me such pleasure before he vanished back into the night. He was off to wander away, free to seek out other women to give them the same joy he'd given me. I would always have this one time, this one night when I pleased him more than any other woman had.

His devilish muse...

My hand absently rubbed at my stomach. In nineteen years, maybe I would tell my daughter about her father while wearing that same smile on my lips that my mother had. There was a part of me that hoped I did conceive a child this night, to have a bit of this man who gave me more pleasure than any other had in my life.

"You are glowing," Cyndi said, shaking her head. "Man, why you? I would love to have been back here with him."

"Sorry," I purred, my voice throaty and smoky. I couldn't help it, my body buzzing.

We re-entered the club, my heel boots thudding on the vinyl flooring. The trance music swelled in volume.

Cyndi gave me a cautious look. "You just be careful with him. He's dangerous. There's something dark about him."

"Yes, there's a shadow in him," I said. I quivered, loving how exciting that made it. "But I wouldn't worry. I don't think I'm ever seeing him again."

Cyndi just shook her head. "We'll see. That look on your face... You just remember this one thing: yeah, he's amazing now, but what if he's like..." She left her words hanging.

I shuddered, hissing, "He's nothing like Tyrone!"

"Tyrone was nothing like Tyrone at first, right?" Cyndi shook her head. "They never are their true selves in the beginning. Just... be careful. Predators can hide behind the hottest of faces."

I gave her a quick hug, squeezing her tight. "Thanks for looking out for me, but I'm a big girl."

She hugged me back, her boobs pressing into my own. I was still sensitive from my orgasm, my nipples tingling as I felt her plump softness. A wave of heat shot through me. I broke away from her, my cheeks flaming. I was shocked by how... intimate hugging my friend felt.

~~*~~

Dean didn't return to the club. Those women who hadn't got a chance to dance with him were all eyeballing the ones who had. Those ladies were floating, having a good time, flirting with guys. It was almost like he was the ultimate wingman, setting up all these girls, getting them excited for a night of passion, and then stepping aside so his friend could jump in and have a good time.

Only Dean had done it for every guy in the bar.

Despite the joy buzzing through me, and the feel of him inside my pussy—it was a naughty thrill to have his cum filling me as I worked, a constant reminder of his passion—my shift began to drag after that. My feet grew sore after hours upon hours of mixing drinks. I was so thankful when final calls were shouted and the last patron left.

It was time for me to cash out.

I always had wads of cash left in my aprons or pockets, tips and payments for drinks that needed to be accounted for. So long as my cash register had all the money in it to equal my sales at the end of the night, I could keep whatever was left over as my tips.

My boss didn't care that it didn't go into the till until right now.

I was counting everything up, when I noticed one of the bills had writing on it. That wasn't terribly uncommon—guys often slipped me tips with their phone numbers written on the bills, which was what I'd found. I frowned at the numbers, staring at the twenty. It had to be one of the two that Dean had given me for the drinks earlier. The writing was crisp and clean, strokes bold. Even though there wasn't a name on it, just the number, I could tell it came from him.

I thought I would never see him again, but he left... this. An invitation.

I bit my lip for a good minute, pondering what to do with it. Then, in a breathless rush, I added his number to my phone, creating a contact for him. I shuddered as I hit save; a ripple of heat washed out of my cum-filled pussy.

I said goodbye to Cyndi and Barley, giving both my co-workers hugs, then I set off into the night, trudging home, my feet killing me. I stopped at the twenty-four-hour convenience store and found the best-looking cat food they had. I went with the dry stuff, paying for it with my tips for the night, and headed home.

Shadow greeted me with an affectionate rub of her whiskered cheek against my heeled boots. I smiled down at her, glad to see her. Her green eyes stared up at me.

"Hey," I said. "I guess you're my cat, huh?"

Her purr rumbled louder. I smiled.

She almost tripped me up as she kept caressing my feet as I headed to the kitchen. Figures—she knew I brought her dinner. I found her a bowl, poured in the cat food, and smiled at her.

"Enjoy," I said, my body exhausted and yet still buzzing from the delight Dean had given me.

I definitely would have that same smile playing on my lips that my mother had when I thought about this night. I would *never* forget Dean even if I never accepted his invitation.

I left Shadow to her dinner and headed to the bathroom. I stripped off my makeup, going through my nightly ritual. Then I headed into my bedroom, taking off my blouse and skirt, wearing only my thong. I removed that, too, shivering at how naughty I felt with his cum leaking out of me. I should definitely clean myself, but I just had this wicked, urgent need to go to bed with him in me.

I hoped to dream about him.

I slipped naked beneath the covers, the sheets rubbing on my flesh like a lover's caress. I shuddered, lying on my side, my breasts piling together. I hugged one of my pillows to my tits, rubbing my cheek against it. My eyes closed.

I sank into dreams.

They were the usual nonsense, those random thoughts that would leave only vague impressions when you awoke the next morning. The ones that quickly faded away as your brain discarded them, not keeping them as anything important or worthwhile.

It was only the special dreams that you remembered. When *my* special dream started, I came aware in a flash, eager for it.

But it wasn't Dean who appeared in my dream. It was the cat, Shadow.

I was lying naked in my bed, the covers thrown off my body. It almost felt like reality, but I just knew that this was a dream. There was something so surreal about it, a glossy shine to the world around me like it was a boudoir photo.

Shadow's triangular ears twitched. Her green, slitted eyes stared up my body as her tongue flicked across her muzzle. A purr rose from her, her whiskers quivering. This strange lust ran through me, this wanton desire that was fed by the cum in my pussy. It was like letting Dean's seed remain inside of me was now fueling this wanton passion for someone. Anyone.

I had to be satiated by a human.

As if in answer to my need, Shadow blurred. She became her namesake, umbral and flowing, swelling larger and larger. Her entire silhouette transformed. The feline vanished, replaced by a figure that was more and more human. Female and naked. Arms reached over her head, fingers sliding through sleek hair. Her back arched, thrusting firm, small breasts at me.

The darkness began melting away, revealing the woman Shadow had become. She was young, my age, her body toned and athletic with light-brown skin that looked soft and silky. She had a lithe grace about her. Her legs were sleek and her hips curvy.

Her eyes were the same green as when she was a cat. Combined with the coffee hue of her skin, it gave her such an exotic look. There was something familiar about this bi-racial woman. Had I seen her at the club? A flash of memory of her dancing with Dean that first night, her flesh melted to his body, jolted through my thoughts.

"Kyrie," Shadow purred as she crawled towards me. Even though she was utterly human now, she still had a feline grace to her movements. "You left him in you." Her nose twitched. "All that wonderful cum. I smelled it. I *need* it."

I shuddered as her fingers caressed my calves, sliding up and up my legs. A wave of heat washed up my thighs. I quivered, wanting this woman to touch me all over. I'd never really been attracted to a girl before. Yes, I could appreciate a beautiful woman, understanding why a guy would find this girl's ass hot or that girl's tits amazing, but I never found it alluring before.

Sexy.

This sudden attraction for the female Shadow had to be the cum in me. It was feeding me Dean's passion. It was like he infected me with his wild lust, making me appreciate the feminine the way he did.

I groaned as dream-Shadow stroked higher and higher up my legs. Her fingers were delicate, her nails coated in a glossy, clear finish. They scraped against my flesh sometimes, adding additional delights racing up my thighs to my pussy.

58

My snatch felt so open, exposed. Shadow's green eyes were fixed right on my sex. Her tongue flicked out across her pink lips. She purred, the sound halfway between feline and human. It was full of hunger. For me. For Dean's seed. She wanted both.

"This is a wicked dream," I groaned as her fingers reach my knees. She traced around them, teasing me.

"Is it a dream?" Shadow asked. Her voice had a smoky, husky quality to it. It was deeper than my own, a delicious contralto.

"It has to be," I moaned as she leaned her head down. Her sleek, black hair fell off her shoulders and swayed about her face. "You're a cat. You can't transform into a woman."

Her tongue licked hot at my thigh right above my knee. I groaned as she fluttered it against my skin, working up my inner flesh. I quivered, my pussy clenching as this beautiful woman lapped closer and closer to my snatch. I couldn't believe I was having such a naughty wet dream.

Her tongue slid past the mid-point of my thigh, so warm and wet. There was a playfulness to the way she would sometimes caress me with fluttering flicks. Other times, she'd kiss and suck, sometimes nibbling. I felt just the lightest touch of her teeth, a naughty reminder to her feline origins.

I groaned and quivered. She stroked her hand down my left thigh, her tongue fluttering down the right. All these naughty sensations built and built in me. The anticipation was almost orgasmic, so similar to a building climax. Maybe I would cum the moment she reached my pussy. A little flash of rapture.

She was four inches away, nearing where my thigh met my pelvis. I quivered, squeezing my tits. I kneaded and massaged them, groaning as she came within three inches. Two. Then she was licking right on the edge of my vulva, my fiery bush caressing her light-brown cheek.

Her lips nuzzled into my cum-stained pubic hair. Her tongue flicked along the edge of my vulva. I groaned, my clit throbbing. My fingernails bit into my tits as I gasped out, "Yes!"

A woman's tongue flicked up my pussy folds. My first lesbian contact, even if it was only in a dream.

A mini-orgasm rippled through me; the tension released. Waves of euphoria washed through me. I groaned, my eyes fluttering while her tongue licked up and down my slit. She gathered Dean's jizz as it leaked out of me, purring as she teased me.

"I love feasting on his seed flowing out of a woman," she moaned. "I love tasting his passion mixed with another. It helps sustain me."

"Uh-huh," I whimpered.

My bed groaned, the mattress springs squeaking beneath me as I humped against her. I ground my pussy on her mouth, working my flesh against hers. I panted and whimpered as the pleasure rippled through me. It was wonderful. Amazing. Her tongue was so gentle, so knowing. It was different from a man's.

From Dean's.

Shadow loved me, her green eyes staring up at me as she probed deeper into my pussy. She scooped out Dean's cum with hunger. My body quivered in shock while true orgasm built inside. My fingers seized my nipples, pinching and rolling them, adding sparks of heat to the delight Shadow generated inside of me.

I whimpered, squeezing my thighs about her face, holding her against my snatch. Her hand slid beneath me, grabbing my rump, kneading and massaging my ass. Her tongue dove deeper into me, swirling against my pussy walls, making me quiver. Her nose nuzzled into my clit, massaging my bud while her tongue probed inside of me, teasing me.

"You're loving this!" I howled. "You're loving licking me clean!"

"Always!" Shadow moaned into my snatch. "This is my Master's jizz. My owner's. I love devouring his seed from a woman. It's my reward!"

This dream was wild.

Shadow's tongue was driving me towards an orgasm. I gasped and bucked, my round breasts jiggling, my nipples shifting in my pinching fingers' grip. I twisted those nubs, adding a splash of delight to the current of pleasure flowing through me.

My orgasm swelled and swelled, her tongue feeding it. She brought me closer to my ecstasy.

She brushed my clit. I gasped as she fluttered against my delicious bud. Her fingers dove into my butt-cheeks as she nibbled on my little nub. She stroked her digits down my crack until she found my asshole.

"Yes, Shadow, yes!" I howled. "Do it!" I felt so wanton. So wild. I just wanted to experience the pleasures in this dream.

She sucked hard on my clit while jamming her finger deep into my asshole. My bowels gripped her thrusting digit as I bucked. Pleasure rippled through me, sparks flaring every time she nursed on my clit.

My orgasm reached its peak. There was no holding it back. I twisted my nipples hard and cried out in wordless pleasure. My bliss detonated through me. My bowels writhed about her probing finger. My pussy convulsed, aching to be filled by Dean's cock.

Her tongue fluttered against my clit, striking new waves of pleasure to flow through me. I bucked and squirmed on my bed, the springs creaking. My thighs gripped Shadow's face, keeping her lips locked on my aching clit. Her finger pumped faster in and out of my asshole, stirring around in my bowels.

My mind drowned beneath waves of ecstasy. I gasped as fuzzy darkness spilled through me. Everything around me became distorted. I felt reality shifting around as I bucked and heaved. Shadow's tongue suddenly grew a little thicker; her cheeks weren't supple, but felt rough.

Like they were a man's stubbly cheeks.

My eyes fluttered as my orgasm died. I blinked in shock, gasping out as the licking tongue drove me towards another orgasm. The silky fabric of my dress rustled as I squirmed. It was bunched around my waist, pulled down to expose my small, quivering breasts.

Those weren't my tits.

I shuddered, realizing that it wasn't Shadow between my thighs now, but Dean. The dream had shifted, and I had become someone else.

"Yes, yes, you're so amazing!" I howled as Dean feasted on my pussy. His nose was pressed not into a fiery bush, but into blonde curls.

I gasped, squeezing these tits, feeling how firm they were. They were just little handfuls, smaller than my own. I was in another woman's body again. Another woman experiencing Dean's passion. I shuddered, humping against him, loving that tongue bathing my pussy. It was those bold strokes, not the playfulness of Shadow, that I felt now.

"I'm so glad you found me," I moaned. "After you danced with me, I didn't think I'd ever see you again."

"How could I stay away from a goddess like you?" Dean growled between licks.

I *was* that blonde in the blue dress he'd danced with at the club. The first woman who'd orgasmed while grinding on him.

I shivered, feeling almost like I was inhabiting her body. Like I'd dreamed myself into her soul. This was such a thrill, the ultimate voyeuristic act. It allowed me to experience Dean's passion again. To relive having my pussy devoured by a master.

Shadow watched me from a doorway, her green eyes intent.

Then pleasure surged through me, drawing my attention back to what was going on. Dean's hands were stroking my thighs, large and rough with callouses, not the gentle, light touch of Shadow. This was a man eating me now. He was driving me wild, sending me towards another orgasm. I shuddered, kneading my smaller breasts. I tweaked the nipples, gasping out my pleasure. Her body was so responsive. Her flesh so in tune with what Dean was doing to her.

"You're going to make me cum!" I moaned. "Make your goddess cum!"

"Yes!" growled Dean. "Shower me with your praise. Bathe me in your adoration, my goddess!"

His hands moved, two thick fingers jamming into the depths of my cunt. I squeezed down on them, reveling in their penetration. Memories of his dick fucking me as he pinned me against the club's wall flashed through my mind.

I bucked on the bed, my head darting to and fro. The room was so different from my own, the furniture expensive, darkly polished. It wasn't purchased at secondhand stores.

I gasped as his plunging fingers drove me wild. They pulled my attention back to the pleasure coursing through me. He sucked hard on my clit and a passionate jolt shot through me. His suction was fiercer than Shadow's. He worshiped my body—the woman in the blue dress's body—with such passion. He drove her—*me!*—wild.

This was incredible.

"Yes, yes, yes!" I howled as my pussy convulsed around his thick fingers. "You're so amazing! I can't believe this! I can't believe you found me!"

His fingers pumped in and out of my convulsing snatch. My pussy spasmed around them, drinking in the silky friction. Wave after wave of pleasure swept through my quivering flesh. This dream was wonderful. I savored it, hoping it wouldn't end. I wanted him to mount me.

To fuck me hard.

"I need you!" I howled. "I need more than your fingers in me. Please! Please!"

He lifted his face, pussy juices dripping down his whisker-shadowed chin. His blue eyes were intense, rippling over me. He was shirtless, his shoulders broad, his pecs and abs sculpted like a bodybuilder's. He rose higher, letting my eyes feast down his body to that hard cock thrusting from his black bush. The massive dick that had stretched me out to my limits. It had made me explode.

"I've been thinking about this cock all night," I moaned. "I felt it when I was grinding on you. You made me cum just from dancing!"

"Now you're eager to find out how hard you'll explode on my dick, aren't you, goddess?" he asked, his eyes intense.

I nodded my head, quivering, my orgasm still spilling through me. It was dying down, but if he thrust his dick in me right now...

"Take me! You promised that you would take me to heaven! I

haven't gotten there!"

"Yet," he growled as he mounted me.

My hands went to his sculpted torso, feeling his strength. My fingernails, painted bright red, scratched at him. I quivered as his dick pressed against the entrance to my pussy. I was so ready for him. So wet and dripping, my orgasm dying down to sputtering coals. I stared into his eyes, pleading.

He thrust into me. He fanned the flames of my orgasm. They roared back to life as my pussy convulsed around his huge dick, welcoming him into my snatch again. I cried out in rapture as my climax surged through me.

My pussy convulsed around his dick, my climax screaming to its full passion as he buried to the hilt in me. He stretched me open. Dean felt even bigger than he had earlier tonight in the alley. This girl had an even tighter pussy than me. He felt incredible in me.

Moaning, my thighs wrapped about him as my scarlet-painted fingernails scratched at his torso. His face contorted in passion, his eyes squeezing shut for a moment. Then they snapped open, brimming with his ardor.

"Feel the strength of my worship, goddess," he growled, drawing back his hips. His cock slid through my tight embrace, the friction stimulating me.

"Yes, yes, I feel it! Worship me!"

He slammed into me again, the bed creaking as he buried to the hilt to me. His balls thwacked into my taint while his pubic bone ground into my clit. Wonderful, delicious sparks exploded through me as he moved his hips, grinding himself against my bud before he drew back. He knew how to use this cock to give me such rapture. I whimpered and groaned, my pussy writhing about him as my orgasms rippled through my body.

Ecstasy splashed against my thoughts.

Little stars burst around him, exploding with the celebration of our passion.

Dean's touch swept up my torso to my small tits. He engulfed them utterly in his hands. His calloused palms rubbed against my hard nipples, sending jolts of tingling rapture shooting down to my orgasming pussy. They fed the churning bliss, mixing with the rapture his cock pumped into me with every thrust.

The orgasm spilled through me, feeding me such rapture. I squeezed my thighs around him, gasping and grunting, loving this. I reveled in the thrill of him plunging into my pussy. He gave me such rapture, such ecstasy. He filled me to the very brim of my femininity. I whimpered, my eyes rolling back in my head.

"Yes, yes, you're taking me to Paradise!" I moaned, the orgasmic rapture washing through my thoughts over and over. "Oh, yes, keep thrusting! You're mine tonight! All mine!"

"Yes," he growled.

His lips nuzzled into my neck, his chest pressing down on me. His hands slipped off my breasts and around my body. He hugged me tight, pulling me against his strong form. His whiskered chin and cheeks rubbed against my silky flesh, smearing my juicy passion against my skin.

I smelled a spicy musk, the scent of this woman's pussy. I loved it, reveling in her—*my*—aroma. I shuddered, humping against him. His dick rammed hard into me. This wonderful rapture swept through me. It consumed me. Dizzying passion whirled through my mind. I clutched him, clawing his back.

My nipples throbbed and ached against his chest. My orgasms spilled faster through me. My pussy convulsed harder. I worshiped his dick as I writhed beneath him. He kissed up to my ear, nibbling on my lobe. He whispered such sweet things.

"My goddess," he growled. "You're taking *me* to Paradise. Oh, my sweet goddess!"

I felt so special. I was his universe right now. I had become this woman, through my dreams, just to be worship by him again. I squeezed my thighs tight about him as my orgasm carried me to such heights. He took me to Paradise like he'd promised. My thoughts drowned beneath the ecstasy.

He pumped in and out of me.

I gasped and bucked beneath him.

My fingernails clawed his back.

I screamed out in ecstasy as stars danced before my vision. My body celebrated him being in me. On me. My nipples rubbed against his chest. His weight felt so wonderful atop me. His balls thwacked into my taint, heavy with his seed.

"Give me your worship!" I howled, delirious with my rapture.

"My sweet goddess!" Dean growled. "There's such sweet solace in your embrace."

He buried to the hilt in me. His hot cum spurted into my pussy. I felt every splash against my spasming cervix. His seed flooded through my orgasming snatch. Waves of rapture shot through me. The wonderful delight spilled ecstasy through my body. I gasped and groaned, crying out as the sweet rapture smothered my mind.

"I'm there! I'm at Paradise!" I screamed at the top of my lungs. "It's amazing!"

My orgasm consumed my mind. My eyes drifted to the right, darkness buzzing along my vision as he grunted, the last of his cum spilling in me.

Shadow, in her human form, watched. Her green eyes were intent, her face serious. Her head cocked to the side. I shuddered, my orgasm peaking and—

I groaned awake. I was on my side again, hugging my pillow to my breasts, my pussy tingling as my convulsions died. There was no cock filling me up. There was no wonderful Dean for my spasming snatch to writhe around.

I groaned, rolling onto my back. I panted, my breasts rising and falling. The dark ceiling of my familiar bedroom almost spun above me. I felt so dizzy from the power of the dream. From the wonder of it. I was enjoying the passion of it.

Even that weird beginning with—

Shadow gave me a start. She sat on the foot of my bed, looking like a cat. She calmly licked her paw. Her ears flickered as her green eyes found mine, the slitted irises reflecting the light bleeding through my curtains. I shuddered, remembering that dream where she'd became a woman and devoured me.

For a moment, I thought she was about to blur into darkness and begin changing.

Instead, she hopped off and darted out of my bedroom, squeezing through my door which was open just enough to let her slender form through. I shook my head. It wasn't like me to leave my door open.

"That was such a weird dream," I murmured. The human version of Shadow had made me cum so hard before bleeding into the delicious dream of Dean.

An impulse seized me. I snagged my phone off my nightstand, yanking the USB charging cord out of it. The screen came to life, battery full. I entered my passcode and found the new contact for Dean. I opened the texting app.

"You're in my head," I typed then added a winky emoji.

I swallowed then hit send.

My message appeared in the yellow bubble at the bottom of the screen. I trembled, waiting to see if he would answer. I gripped my phone in my hand, my heart drumming as a nervous writhe twisted through me. Was it too soon to send Dean a message? Should I have waited? Played cool? Would he think I was desperate for his attention now?

It had only been a few hours...

Just when I thought I'd made a mistake, that I was too eager, a blue text bubble appeared at the bottom of my screen, sliding up my own message to show his.

"You better watch out, then," Dean replied, adding his own flirty, winky emoji to the message. *"There's all sorts of* terrible *things I could do to you now."*

I shuddered, my fingers blurring as I typed, *"Like what?"*

"Well, you got that great ass. Just begging for pleasure."

"Anal?" I shuddered, my pussy clenching. I'd never let that bastard Tyrone have that treat. Even when he would beat me for refusing. But for Dean...

"We can try that," Dean texted back. *"You just have a delicious*

rump. It's just begging to be spanked."

A hot shudder rippled through me.

"Just picture yourself, kneeling on your bed, me behind you. In you. And then that CRACK!"

My ass clenched, almost feeling the stinging impact. My fingers typed, *"Yes!"* I added a splooshing water emoji. *"That does sound just terrible. Such a bad man trying to spank me. I'm a good girl."*

"Such a good girl. You fell to your knees, sucked my cock, and then exploded on my dick not long ago."

"All good girls suck cock, don't you know that?" I wrote, loving this. I'd never sexted with a guy before. I rubbed my thighs together, my pussy feeling so juicy.

"Yes, you're definitely a good girl. But even good girls need to be spanked. They're the ones who want to be the naughtiest, after all." He added a winky emoji.

"Yes!!!" I texted back with feverish intensity.

My clit was on fire. I shoved my hand between my thighs and rubbed my soaking flesh. I was still burning from the passion of my dream. The excitement of his cock combined with the excitement of sexting with him. It sent me over the edge in a moment.

I clutched my phone tight as ripples of delight washed through me. Not a powerful orgasm, but a nice, little dessert after the feast I had had. The bliss flooded out of my pussy and through my body. I whimpered on the bed, my phone shaking in my hand.

A beep echoed from my phone as I writhed through my rapture.

"You're being bad right now, aren't you?" Dean texted.

Did he know I was cumming? No, he couldn't have.

I shivered on the bed as my pleasure peaked in me. I whimpered, rubbing my thighs tight together as the pleasure buzzed through me. Little stars danced before my eyes. I struggled to type with one hand while I came down from my climactic rapture.

"Maybe I was," I sent. *"Maybe you should spank me the next time we meet."*

He winked at me.

My breasts rose and fell as my orgasmic delight faded away. I thought about the dream as I struggled to gather my thoughts. Did I really imagine I was someone else? Had I really occupied another woman's body during my dream?

Curious, I typed, *"Were you with another woman tonight? Were you naughty?"*

"Why? Jealous?" was his response.

I thought about it. I didn't feel any anger or annoyance. Though I wanted him, ached for him, I felt like he was more than one woman—more than I—could ever handle. Perhaps I should be jealous, but...

"Did she cum as hard as I did?" I sent.

"A gentleman doesn't tell," he replied.

"But you're not a gentleman," I typed back right away. *"You're a wanderer."*

"I made a lot of women cum tonight. You saw me dancing. But none of them were as sweet or as tasty as you."

I quivered at those words. I was better than all of them, even that blonde woman. Was he in her bathroom right now, sexting with me while she quivered on her bed aching for him to return to her?

"Good," I sent.

I smiled and sank back onto my pillows. I set my phone my on my nightstand, sleep weighing heavily down on me. I rolled over onto my side, my thighs sticky with my own juices, and fell into pleasant, if normal, dreams.

~~*~~

Dean Walker

I smiled, staring at my phone. She was a naughty thing. There was a playfulness that was hidden beneath the professional demeanor she wore at the club. I liked that. I was glad I found her. She was making this mission so much more enticing.

69

My phone beeped. I received a text not from Kyrie, but from Elizabeth. I switched to her message, smiling at the purple bubble around her text. I didn't choose the color, but it fit her in a way.

"Master, she is definitely leaving her body while dreaming," read Elizabeth's message. "She inhabited another woman's soul. A woman caught up in rapture."

I frowned as I kept reading. It was confirmation. Kyrie was like me. She was a half-devil. A cambion.

Chapter Six: Investigations

Kyrie Hope

I kept glancing at my phone as I walked to work the next day, eager to see Dean. I read through our flirty texts, loving how wicked they were. We did such naughty things in my dreams, and now he promised to do more to me in real life. I was eager for him to spank me as he took me from behind.

I was even intrigued by the possibility of anal sex with him.

My heeled boots thudded on the cement sidewalk as I strutted towards the Green Eye Delight, my jeans skirt swishing about my thighs. It was the shortest skirt I owned. It hugged my ass and rode up so high I was a little afraid I might show off my panties. I had a red thong on beneath, something naughty and wicked.

Something I hoped Dean would love when he saw me tonight.

My breasts jiggled the stretchy V-neck top I wore. The deep, royal blue fabric outlined my breasts. I should've worn a bra with it because my nipples were totally on display. I just felt so wicked. I so wanted to see Dean. Wanted him to see me like this. To be his goddess.

His devilish muse.

I almost sent him a text asking if he would be at the club

tonight. I just had a feeling he would be. For whatever reason, the wanderer had found something to stick around for. I felt it was me. I had... sparked something in him.

I know he definitely sparked something in me. There was a fire raging inside of me that I couldn't put out.

I swept into the club past Jerome, the bouncer. The beefy, African-American guy in a tight, black t-shirt with SECURITY printed on the front nodded to me. He swept open the door for me. Like the night before, the club was brimming with women all eager to see Dean. The music thudded, my head nodding to the beat as I went into the back and dropped off my purse. My black half-apron donned, I joined Cyndi up front.

There was a wicked grin on my friend's face. Her hazel eyes flicked up and down, inspecting me as she adjusted her red-rimmed glasses. Her tits quivered in a scoop-neck blouse, the black material hugging tight to her large tits. She wore a skirt that was somehow shorter than mine, a black sheath that hugged about her pale thighs and cupped her rump.

"Trying to attract Dean yourself?" I asked.

"Why should you get all the fun?" she responded, a smile playing on her lips. She rubbed at her side, scratching at an itch. "God, I'm so jealous of you. You're dreaming about him *and* fucking him behind the club."

I leaned in and, in a conspiratorial tone, whispered, "He promised to spank my ass next time. It sounds so naughty."

Cyndi nodded her head, her blonde curls swaying about her face. This strange expression crossed her features, almost looking sage, as she said, "Yes, little grasshopper, it is a delight that you shall enjoy."

Laughter burst from me.

"Hello," growled a gravely voice. "If you two are done giggling?"

I spun on my heels, my cheeks burning. "I'm so sorry, I..."

My words trailed off as I stared at the two figures at the bar. They weren't here for partying. The man was older, dressed in a cheap, mustard suit, his brown tie half undone. He had a scar that ran across his temple before plunging into his iron-gray hairline, leaving a smooth line deep where no hair grew at all. It reached past his ear. The woman was younger, her skin dusky like she was Middle-Eastern, her black hair pulled up into a no-nonsense bun. She wore a beige trench coat over a white blouse buttoned all the way to her throat. Both of them produced badges, flashing their police credentials.

"I'm Detective Miller," the gruff cop said, then he nodded to the woman, "and she's Detective Jones."

"We just need to ask a few questions," Detective Jones said, her words chilly.

A nervous twist rippled through my stomach. "Sure. About what?" I swallowed. "Love to help the police."

Cyndi sidled up to me, nodding her head.

Detective Miller produced a manila folder from beneath his mustard suit jacket and flipped it open on the darkly polished bar. He spread out pictures of two women; one had brown hair, a smile on her face, dressed in a white tennis outfit. The other was a blonde, beaming in proud delight as she stood in her graduation robes, looking so young and happy.

"You recognize either of these two girls?" Miller asked.

I frowned, staring at them. My eyes flicked back and forth, racking my brain for all the women that come and go at the club. So many passed through those doors, dancing, drinking, flirting. Then I noticed the tattoo on the brunette's inner forearm.

A tiger.

My stomach clenched while flashes of my dream from two nights ago flickered through my thoughts. I'd reached up with that very arm to clutch at Dean as he pistoned his cock in and out of my body—no, it was *her* body!

My eyes darted over to the blonde. She was petite and a few years younger in the picture than the woman I saw dancing with Dean last night. Than the woman who cried out as Dean took her to Paradise in my dreams last night.

"Yeah," I said slowly. "I've seen them in the club." I tapped the brunette's picture. "I saw her here two nights ago, and I saw the blonde last night."

Cyndi gasped, "The girl with the tattoo was here? Right, right, she was that busty brunette in the red mesh mini dress with the square neckline." Then Cyndi's eyes slid to the blonde. "And she was the one wearing a blue V-necked mini dress with the narrow shoulder straps."

"You're sure?" asked Detective Jones. "They were at the club on those nights?"

I nodded my head. "Yeah, pretty sure."

Detective Miller glanced to Cyndi. "You're pretty sure on the dresses."

"Because my tits would look amazing in either of those dresses," said Cyndi.

"She always notices what everyone wears," I explained. "She's got a memory like a hawk for it."

Cyndi tapped the side of her head, "It's like encyclopedia fashion up here. The only thing I'm good at."

"You see them with anyone last night? Dancing, or maybe someone they left with?" Detective Jones asked. "Or someone bothering them?"

My stomach sank more. "Why? Did something... happen to them?"

"Did you see any guys harassing them, or just spending time with them?" the gruff voice of Detective Miller asked.

My entire body shuddered. There was only one reason they would be asking these sort of questions. "Are they...? Are they dead?"

"Yes," Detective Jones said, her words clipped. "Now, we need to know if they left the club with anyone?"

"I... I don't remember," I said, shaking my head. I was so confused about my dreams. How could I have imagined myself as them and then...? I shivered, wondering if I was dreaming about them right before... "When did they... die?"

Jones glanced at her partner. The older detective shrugged his shoulders, rustling his ugly jacket. Detective Jones glanced at me and said, "Brittany Morals died last night or early this morning and Rebecca Abrams the night before."

I had names to go with the women I'd become. I trembled while the world felt off-kilter, like its foundations had sunk in one corner, giving everything a surreal, nightmarish angle.

"Well, there was one guy that every woman here was after," Cyndi said. "A real hunk. I mean, look at how I'm dressed. I was hoping to catch his eye tonight."

My gaze shot to her. "What? No. He had nothing to do with it."

"Stranger?" asked Detective Miller. "Who are you talking about?"

"His name's Dean, right?" Cyndi asked me.

I nodded my head. "Dean Walker. He was in here the last two nights, but I didn't see him leave with them." Just dreamed he was with them. "Or with anyone."

This horror spilled through me. Why had I had a dream about them? What did it mean?

"Kyrie's pretty taken with the guy," Cyndi said. "She hooked up with him last night during her break. They went out back and did it."

My cheeks burned despite the queasiness writhing through my stomach. "But Dean didn't hurt me or anything. I mean..." My eyes stared at the two dead women's pictures. They were both smiling. They had experienced rapture in my dreams. Dean had given them bliss like he'd given me. "I can't believe he had anything to do with... this."

"What does he look like?" Detective Jones asked, pulling out a notepad from her pocket.

"God, just a hunk," Cyndi said, her voice throaty. "Tall and broad shouldered, with that sort of brooding, French passion to his features. You know, the sort of heavy eyebrows. The chiseled chin. I thought he'd stepped off a romance novel cover. And those eyes..." Cyndi shuddered, her breasts swaying in her low-cut blouse.

"They're so blue. Vivid. When he looks at you, it feels like he's seeing into your soul. Into what you crave. That's why there's all these women here. They're all hoping to dance with him again. To go home with him."

"Yeah, but I'm sure he went home alone," I said.

Detective Miller produced another manila envelope. He spread out a group of about seven or eight photos, all of different men. My eyes flicked from one to the other: they were all young. Dark hair. Some were security camera pictures, others looked like they might be mugshots, and... One was of Dean—a little grainy, but it was him.

"You see the guy you're talking about in these photos?" Detective Miller asked. "Huh?"

Cyndi pushed up her glasses then said, "That's him." She tapped Dean's photo. "Right, Kyrie?"

I felt both the cops' eyes lock on me. Pressure weighed down on me. "Yeah, that's him."

"Are you in contact with him?" Detective Miller asked me. "I mean, if you hooked up with him you must have a number or something."

"Yeah, we exchanged some texts at, I don't know, around three this morning."

"So you have his phone number?" Detective Jones asked, an eagerness entering her voice.

Feeling like I had no choice, I fetched my phone from my purse in the back, my thoughts skipping as I struggled to understand this new world I lived in. I found the number and gave it to the detectives. It went down into Jones's notebook.

"But I still don't think he did anything," I said. "He doesn't seem like the type."

"This man was photographed leaving Brittany Morals's apartment at 3:46 AM. He was caught on her building's security camera," Jones said, tapping the picture of Dean. She produced another folder full of more photographs. There was Dean entering the building. In another, he was in the hallway knocking on a door.

The next, the door was open, and I could see the blonde woman just in frame.

"The next person who entered her apartment, her sister, found her dead. We have similar photos at Rebecca Abrams's apartment. This man was the last person seen alive with either of these women."

Detective Miller's eyes were hard. "If you see this Dean Walker, call us immediately." He produced a business card and set it on the bar. "And call the police. He's dangerous."

He slid the card towards me. I trembled as I picked it up, my fingers stroking the cream-colored stock. It was plain with black text printed on it. His name and number, nothing more. I swallowed, not wanting to believe it, but...

Was Dean texting me after he'd killed Brittney?

~~*~~

Dean Walker never showed up at the club. I worked in a daze, unable to process what I'd learned. How to reconcile a murderer with the man who gave me such passion in the alley. He'd found me in such a vulnerable place, isolated and alone, and could have hurt me the way he supposedly harmed the other girls. Instead, he'd given me such pleasure.

Just like in those dreams, to those girls. It didn't make any sense.

Of course, Tyrone didn't seem like an abusive asshole with a temper who'd beat me when I'd first met him. I thought I had grown better at detecting dangerous men. That I'd learned from Tyrone, discovered what to look out for. The possessiveness. The controlling impulses. I didn't get that from Dean. He just wanted to give me rapture. I felt like I could have said no at any time. That Dean would have stopped.

Instead, I was eager to do things with him.

Just like the women I dreamed about. What was up with those dreams, anyway? Why did I have them?

I couldn't come up with any possible reason why I would

dream about those two girls with Dean *before* their murders. It shouldn't be possible for me to do that. It was almost like I was... psychic or something. But that wasn't real. Miracles and the supernatural and ESP were all fakes. None of that had ever been proven. It was always debunked. They were claims used by fraudsters who wanted to take advantage of grieving people and pretend to speak to their loved ones and stuff like that.

But... I had those dreams...

"You okay?" Cyndi asked as we were getting ready to leave. "You still look... stunned."

"Yeah. Blame me?" I asked.

She enfolded me in her arms, squeezing me tight. "No, I can't. He's dangerous. Maybe... maybe you should stay at my place tonight."

I hesitated before saying, "No, no. I'm fine. I have a deadbolt. And..." I didn't want to mention the .380 pistol I kept in my nightstand's drawer. "I'll be fine. I can take care of myself."

"Are you sure?" she asked. "I don't want to worry about you."

"It's not like he knows where I live," I said.

"As far as you know."

I shivered. "It's just... I can't believe *he* would do that!"

"Because you had a few dreams?" asked Cyndi. Her hazel eyes speared into mine. "It was those girls, wasn't it? The ones you dreamed about him being with. The ones who...?"

I nodded my head. "What does that mean?"

"That we're all connected." Her fingernails bit into my bare shoulders as she clutched me tight. "We all forge these bonds with each other's soul. Unseen, unknown, ethereal. They're made of jealousy, lust, friendship, love, hatred. All of them extend beyond the physical world. They bind us together. Some are as strong as steel chains, others are as thin as a strand of hair and just as easy to snap. Maybe... you just followed one to their dreams."

"Why would I have followed one?" I asked.

"Because of him. Because you wanted to be with him, and he went to those other women."

"I'm not jealous!" I objected. "Besides, *I* was with him. Last night. He didn't do anything to harm me. He just loved me."

"He loved those women in your dreams, too," she said. "Even monsters can love. Doesn't mean they won't hurt you in the end."

"I'll be fine," I insisted. My back straightened with pride at how far I'd come since Tyrone. I was independent. I was strong. I would take care of myself.

"Okay, but let's walk home together as far as we can. Okay?"

I nodded. "Sure."

I finished cashing out, my tips safely tucked in my purse, then Cyndi and I strolled out of the Green Eye Delight. The bouncer, Jerome, nodded to us. "I haven't seen that bastard, ladies."

"Thanks, Jerome" I said, giving him a smile.

The burly, Black man gave me a fierce nod.

Cyndi and I walked down the dark sidewalk, arms entwined. It felt nice having my friend beside me, our heels clicking in the near-silence. I hated walking home through this neighborhood most times, but that night... my eyes were so aware of all the shadows. I kept flicking to them, studying them. I remembered how Dean seemed to just melt out of them. The shadows had embraced him like they were his lover. A nervous tremble built and built in me the closer we came to where we would have to part.

After five minutes or so, we reached the intersection. My apartment was still a few blocks straight ahead while Cyndi's was five blocks to our left. Maybe I should go home with her...

No. I could see the neon-bright sign glowing in the dark—Coat of Arms Apartments—shining ahead. It was a beacon leading me home. I could do this. "Night, Cyndi."

"You text me the moment you're behind your locked door," Cyndi said. "Promise me. I don't want him getting you. You're *my* friend."

I beamed at her. "I will!"

We exchanged a quick, fierce hug before breaking apart. I crossed the street as she scurried off towards her own apartment, her blonde hair bouncing about her shoulders, her heels clicking while my boots thudded. I reached the other side, staring ahead, the sign beckoning me home. I would be there in a minute or two. I clutched my purse tight, taking the longest strides I could.

My breasts jiggled thanks to my hurried pace. It was practically a run. This nervous confusion swelled and swelled in me. Did I want to see Dean? To confront him? I had to know. He couldn't be this monster that the police alleged.

I couldn't be *that* bad at judging men?

Had I learned nothing from Tyrone?

A block away from my apartments, the shadows rippled. He melted out of them wearing his leather jacket, a black t-shirt stretched tight across his chest. His jeans rasped together as he stopped before me. He held his hands out to his side, down low, not threatening.

"My devilish muse," he said, his voice that deep rumble that ignited such a fire in me.

Despite the fear, or maybe because of it, I wanted to dart to him and throw my arms around him. To kiss him. I wanted to take that risk, to give myself to that pleasure. It was incredible what he gave me last night, in my dreams. My entire body quivered, my flesh on fire. My pussy soaked my thong as I let out a wanton groan.

With the greatest effort, my hands clenched into balled fists, I resisted taking those two steps and embracing him.

"Have you always dreamed of other people?" he asked me, his blue eyes reflecting the street light overhead.

His question caught me off-guard. "What?" I stammered. "How do you know...?"

"Kyrie, do you always dream you are other people, or is this a new thing?" he asked again, his words sending a shiver down my spine.

"How do you...?" I trembled, my heart racing. What was going on? My life felt topsy-turvy all of a sudden.

He took a step closer to me. I could feel the heat radiating off his body. "You dreamed, last night, didn't you? That you were another woman?"

"A dead woman," I said, the trembles increasing in intensity. My booted feet shifted on the concrete sidewalk.

"But she wasn't dead when you dreamed of her, was she? This has happened before? Did it happen with the other one?"

I studied his face. This was the monster the police said murdered those two girls, but I didn't see anything evil in his expression. His blue eyes were so soulful, they were full of begging need. He wanted me to understand. He was so strong, but not dangerous in a violent way, only in a soul-consuming, passionate way.

He could grab me in an instant. He could seize me, overpower me in a heartbeat. I clutched my purse, trembling, the musk of his leather jacket filling my nose. His presence was so immediate. He felt more real than the street we stood on.

I just wanted to kiss him again. To experience that rapture again.

"Only those two times," I said, wanting to back away from my lusts, wanting to step forward towards him. "Did you... kill them?"

"You think I killed them?" he asked.

His right hand moved, not fast, but slow as he reached for me. He was giving me a chance to retreat. I could do that; I could dart across the street and make a mad dash for my apartment. Maybe I could outrun him? I used to be fast when I ran track and field in school.

His hand cupped my cheek, his rough fingers warm and gentle. His thumb stroked along my cheekbone while a rush of fire shot through me. I quivered, shuddering. His blue eyes were so intense, wanting to swallow my soul.

"Do you trust these dreams you're having?" he asked. "Do you think they show the truth?"

"Were you with those women?" I asked.

"Something was with them," he said, his thumb still caressing me. "That's what Elizabeth told me. Something with my face, but it wasn't me. It's a... complication."

I wanted to believe that, but it was Dean in my dreams. Felt like him. The Dean in my dreams fucked with the same passion that he'd given me in the alley. He loved those women; how could he have hurt them? He was gentle as he touched me despite his strength. His head leaned down, his lips nearing mine. I couldn't help myself, I arched my head, lifting my lips to meet his.

His mouth melted against mine. I shuddered as I felt the intensity of it. His lips were hot, searing me with his ardor. I quivered, my fingers clenching at my purse, fighting to let go. To embrace him. To let him just ravish me. I wanted that. I ached to have him take me hard right here on the sidewalk.

I yearned for him to spank my ass as he fucked me from behind.

He was the last person to be seen with those women.

Was I next? I wanted to invite him up to my apartment, to spend the night with him. To take that chance. This dangerous exhilaration mixed with the lust. It sweetened my desire. Sharpened it. I felt like my passion was honed to a razor's edge of ecstasy.

Or agony.

Just as I quivered, on the verge of surrendering and inviting him inside, an alley cat yowled.

The sudden sound startled us both. Dean wrenched his lips from mine and flicked his eyes up the street. "Gehenna's fires!" he snarled. "Trust your dreams, Kyrie. They're real, but they're also deceptive. People can lie in them just like they can in the waking world."

"What?" I asked before he flowed into the shadows that he came from. He vanished into the night.

I quivered, shuddering.

Then a bright light illuminated me from behind. I gasped, spinning around to see a car approaching, a spotlight blazing from its side. I held up my hand to shield my blinded eyes from the glare and realized it was a police cruiser. It pulled up alongside me, the window buzzing down. In the passenger seat was a young, bluff-faced cop, his hair buzzed to a flattop.

"You okay, ma'am?" he asked, thrusting his arm out the

window, clutching the side of his door. "It's Kyrie, right?"

I nodded, my body a mix of lusty fire and fearful ice.

"Detective Jones asked us to drive by your apartment and check up on you." He glanced at me. "You okay?"

I swallowed, trembling. What should I do? "He..."

If my dreams were true, then he was with those women before they died just like the detectives said. Could I trust Dean? Was he trying to seduce me into...

Fear won.

"He was just here."

"The suspect?" the cop asked, his face growing dark.

I pointed at the shadowy alley. "He went that way."

Chapter Seven: Confusion

Kyrie Hope

I was exhausted when I finally finished talking to Detectives Miller and Jones. They interviewed me for an hour, questioning me over and over about what Dean said, what he meant by my dreams. I just told the pair that I was having sex dreams of Dean. That he got in my head.

Which he had.

I told them how he was waiting for me. How he'd confused me. When he was kissing me, it felt like I could trust him.

I still felt like I could trust him. But...

Tyrone lurked in my psyche. The first year of our relationship, I thought he loved me. The first time he hit me, I thought it was a mistake. A one-time thing. I *believed* him when he said it wouldn't happen again. And it didn't for a while. A few months later, however, he struck me again after losing his temper. Then the beatings came more and more often.

Bit by bit, I realized he was a snake. That he'd deceived me.

Was Dean doing the same thing to me?

The way he touched me, stroked me...

Though he said that my dreams were true, he implied that they were also a lie. What did that mean?

My brain was fried as I stumbled into my apartment. I closed the door behind me, leaning against it before I locked the deadbolt and slid the chain home. Shadow strolled up to me and rubbed her whiskered cheek affectionately against my heeled boots.

I bent down and stroked her soft, warm fur, staring into her green eyes. Her gaze felt so comforting. It was almost like she was promising that she would protect me. I knew it was ridiculous, but I couldn't help bending down and planting a quick kiss on her muzzle. Her whiskers brushed my lips. Then she shook her head, her ears twitching.

With my mind fried, I found myself giggling at the sight.

My frazzled mirth trailed off into hiccuping silence as the reality sank in again. I shuddered, my eyes fluttering. I didn't know what to believe. What to think. What was real? What was truth and what were lies? Did Dean come close to killing me tonight, or was I mistaken about what I'd witnessed in my dreams? Were the police wrong, too? They had those photos. Security footage. Those were actual proof that Dean had been with those women before they'd died.

I stumbled down the hallway to my bathroom. I stared at myself in the mirror, my cheeks flushed, my features appealing with the makeup on. I appeared almost whorish. I dressed up for tonight, wearing my naughtiest clothing, eager to have a night of passion with him. And now...

I wiped at the makeup with a triangular sponge, the rubbing alcohol stripping it away. In minutes it was gone, my natural beauty revealed. I really didn't need much at all, just emphasizing parts of me: cheekbones, eyes, the plumpness of my lips. Just enhancing me to make myself a little more... inviting.

In my bedroom, I stripped naked, grabbed a clean pair of panties to slip on, and snagged a long t-shirt to wear. I pulled the covers over my body, closed my eyes, and felt myself drifting off to sleep except...

What if I dreamed?

That snapped me wide awake.

What if I dreamed of another girl experiencing her final moments of passion with Dean? I didn't want that. Why was I having these dreams?

Why did I have this connection with him?

~~*~~

My brain felt like mush the next day. Rest did not come easily. Every time I started to drift down, a spike of fear shot through me. I was terrified of what I would see. That it would happen again. I had this strange thought that if I didn't sleep, no one would die.

I don't know when I succumbed to exhaustion, maybe it was around five or six, but I slipped into a fitful doze that lasted until the mid-afternoon. My alarm clock's beeping woke me up for work. My eyelids were heavy. I had a slight headache squeezing my skull.

I didn't wear a skirt to the club today. I went with jeans like normal, and definitely not my tightest pair. My blouse was more conservative, a scoop-neck, green top. My red hair was brushed out to its normal curly sheen. I didn't apply much makeup, just enough to hide the bags underneath my eyes.

The detectives were waiting for me when I arrived at my job.

"Have you caught him?" I asked, not sure what I wanted their answer to be. I still wasn't sure about Dean. The way he kissed me...

"Not yet, but he won't evade us forever," Detective Miller said, his voice a low growl.

"Patrols didn't see anything around your apartment either," said Detective Jones, her name at such odds to her dusky skin. "But we think he might still try to make contact with you."

I nodded my head. I wasn't surprised.

"We're going to have a few plainclothes cops in the club pretending to be patrons. We're going to pull back any patrols or extra security. Try to make it look like nothing special's going on. We think he'll show up tonight. Either way, just act like everything is normal, do your job, and know that there will be at least two cops in sight of you. Okay?"

I nodded my head, giving them a grateful smile.

Detective Jones grabbed my shoulder, the smile on her face looking at odds with her cold expression, her black hair still pulled back in that severe bun. "We're going to catch him, Kyrie. We won't let him hurt you, okay?"

Why would he hurt me? "Thank you."

"Damn, you get all the attention," Cyndi said after the detectives left. She was wearing another scandalous outfit—thigh-high boots and a leather skirt so short that the bottom cheeks of her ass peeked out, flashing the lacy red of her panties. With it, she wore a leather top that was a mix between a bra and a corset. It lifted her lush breasts into two jiggling mounds. Her blonde hair swept about her face, her hazel eyes mischievous behind her glasses.

"Are you trying to bait him out yourself?" I asked.

"I'm supposed to act normal," Cyndi said. "Dressing like this *is* normal for me." Her eyes flicked up and down. "But... even for you, that's a little drab."

I faked an easy manner, hiding the turmoil in my guts as I rolled my eyes and said, "Let's get the bar ready. We still have a job to do."

Cyndi laughed. "Always so professional." She shook her head. "Too bad this Dean turned out to be a monster because he was turning you into a fun girl."

My cheeks warmed.

As we settled into the routine, the tension inside of me dwindled. I still wasn't sure if I was afraid of Dean harming me, or him getting caught by the cops. I was still in this strange denial. My dreams, the photos, were all *proof* that he, at the very least, was the last person to be seen with those women alive. If he didn't kill them, who did?

The way he kissed me, the gentleness of his touch, the fact he *could have* done something to me seemed contrary to everything else. It was almost like he was trying to prove his innocence to me the night before, but that cop showed up and forced him to retreat.

If Dean was smart, he would wander far away from this, but...

He didn't seem the type to flee if he was innocent.

"Oh, she's got a cute dress, doesn't she?" said Cyndi, nudging my arm with her elbow. "That green would look amazing on me, and on you, with your red hair... You'd be stunning!"

I followed her gaze to a blonde woman in a very short mini-dress dancing with a guy, her rump shaking back and forth, her golden hair bouncing.

"That skirt's too short for me," I said.

Cyndi rolled her eyes.

It seemed like tonight she was trying to point out girls and their dresses more often than normal. It was like she was trying to distract me from what was going on. In her own way, she was trying to be the best friend that she could. I really appreciated it, even if I wasn't in the mood to be envious of other girls' outfits.

"Look at that redhead in that black dress," she moaned. "You'd look so killer in it. And me... My tits would just be falling out of it."

Another time, she squealed, "Oh, my God, Kyrie, do you see that creamy, orange dress that brunette is wearing? It has sequins. My ass would look so amazing in it."

I just shook my head. Cyndi would be Cyndi.

The night dragged on and on. A quivering tension filled the air. It was clear after a few hours that Dean wasn't showing up. He knew the police were looking for him, knew that they were watching me. He wasn't dumb enough to come here.

I tried to stay relaxed, to smile and be a good bartender. I hoped my customers didn't notice that there was anything wrong. Everyone seemed to be having fun, even if the women all looked a tad disappointed. The guys were happier, though.

The tips were better.

I felt terrible for thinking that. Two women were dead. I had to remember that. I needed to understand what was going on, but what else could I do besides being bait? I wanted to prevent more from suffering. But I was just a bartender. A girl on the run from her abusive boyfriend.

If Tyrone discovered I was here...

I didn't want to start over again. I liked Cyndi. I liked my apartment. I guess I could take Shadow with me, but I didn't want to pack up and move for a third time. This last year was a nightmare. I was only now getting back on my feet, building something new, and...

I was being selfish again.

How could I help stop this?

I had no idea.

The end of the night came, the undercover cops hanging out at the bar appearing tired themselves. I cashed out, gathered up my purse, and was ready to go home. I had my own police escort. One of the undercover cops, a handsome man named Darren, gave me a ride home in his unmarked car.

"There's going to be a detail watching you," he said when he pulled up before my apartment building. "See." He nodded towards the patrol car parked along the curb in front of my building. "Just to be safe. So you don't have anything to worry about."

"Thanks," I said, giving him a smile. I felt like I should smile, to show my appreciation. But what if Dean *was* innocent?

There had to be some way to help prove that. Maybe through my dreams? Unless my dreams would prove the opposite? Prove that he was guilty.

I trudged up the stairs, my feet aching as always. Shadow was there to greet me when I entered my apartment. She was purring, rubbing against my heeled boots. She somehow knew I needed affection. Animals were empathetic. I don't know what led her to be waiting on my doormat, why she chose me to be her new owner, but I was grateful.

Even if I did have that naughty dream of her turning into that sexy, dusky-skinned woman.

"How was your day?" I asked. "Hope it wasn't nearly as stressful as mine?"

She meowed as she followed me towards the bathroom to strip off my makeup.

"Sounds interesting," I said, pretending we were having a conversation. "Mine was just boring tedium."

I chatted with her as I stripped off my makeup, the scent of rubbing alcohol filling the air. She followed me into my bedroom this time. I didn't mind. I left the door open just enough so she could leave if she wanted. I didn't have any problem stripping naked before her; she was a cat, after all, despite that weird sex dream I'd had.

Dressed in my sleepwear, I slipped beneath my covers. Shadow hopped onto the bed and curled up on my other pillow, her green eyes facing me. She became a fuzzy ball of black as she settled down. Her tail twitched behind her. I smiled, feeling safe. Watched over.

Didn't the Egyptians believe that cats protected their souls or something?

Maybe it was true. Maybe I didn't have to be afraid of falling asleep tonight. I was so tired, exhausted from getting little rest the previous night.

My eyes, growing heavier and heavier, drifted closed.

The dreams came. Nonsense mostly. I didn't know how long I drifted between strange fantasies. It was all going fine until it all felt suddenly so real. So immediate. This was a *special* dream.

"Oh, my God, how did you find me?" I moaned. I was sitting on a couch in a living room, my creamy, orange skirt hiked up my lush thighs and bunched around my waist. A skimpy, black thong I'd never owned cupped my juicy pussy.

Dean was kneeling between my spread-open legs, staring up at me with those hungry, blue eyes.

"You're my goddess," he growled, his hands stroking up my thighs, reaching for the dainty thong. "I've been wanting to worship you since I saw you tonight."

Tonight? When did Dean see this woman? I recognized the orange, creamy hue of this dress and the flashing sequins. I shifted my head just enough to see the brown curls. I definitely saw this woman at the club.

Panic shot through me even as I moaned out in a wanton voice,

"I'm so glad. I was so disappointed when you didn't show up at the club tonight. I wanted to dance with you again. I came so hard last time."

"You're going to cum even harder tonight," he growled.

Why did I keep saying these naughty words? Why did I shudder and groan as he grabbed the waistband of my thong? I had to find clues to who I was. I lifted my ass up, letting him rip the thong down my thighs. Despite the fear in me, I couldn't stop this from happening. It was like...

I wasn't really in control.

I just *felt* like I was. But I really was this woman, witnessing her experiences, inhabiting her soul. Whoever the brunette in the creamy orange dress was, this was her life, her living room, which meant...

I had to do something to save her.

This was *really* happening, so I had to make sure she would survive. I had to protect her. Panic flooded through my soul even as Dean drew the panties farther and farther down my legs. They were past my knees, my pussy feeling so wet, so eager for him.

"Eat me," I moaned in throaty passion.

"I will gladly worship you, my goddess!" he groaned, sounding just like he had in the alley. In all the dreams.

The scratch of his whiskers on my inner thighs as he leaned in to lick me felt like the real Dean, not a lie. The flick of his tongue through the folds of my pussy was so bold. So like him. He brushed my clit, sending rapture shooting through me.

My eyes squeezed shut.

No, no, no! I screamed in my thoughts. *Don't close your eyes. I need to see what's around you.*

The pleasure felt incredible as he licked again, his stubble rasping on my pussy lips. They were shaved bare. I quivered, my breasts swaying in the dress. My toes curled in my heels.

Open our eyes and—

Her eyes snapped open. She shot her hands down to grab Dean's thick mane of shaggy hair. She gripped him as she shuddered, his tongue fluttering through her folds.

"Worship me!" I moaned as I struggled to move my eyes. My head. I had to find something that could identify who she was. Where she lived.

"I'll feast on you, my goddess!" Dean groaned between hot licks, pleasure shooting through me.

I saw something out of the corner of my eye.

An envelope!

It had to have her address on it. I just couldn't quite focus on the letters. I could just see it out of the corner of my eye. *You have to move your head*, I screamed in my thoughts even as I trembled, humping against Dean's hungry mouth. Such rapture swept through my body with his tongue's every stroke. *Please, please. You have to move your head.*

"Oh, God, this is even better than I imagined!" I moaned out loud. "This is even better than masturbating to you! I fingered myself so many times last night, aching for you, imagining what this would be like. You're so much better!"

I know it's amazing, but you have to move your head! I roared. *The envelope's right there. Please, please, move your head!*

Maybe the woman I was dreaming as heard me, or maybe it was just the pleasure coursing through her body that caused her to turn her head, but she did it. It felt so natural, like I was moving her. I knew I wasn't in control, that it was just an illusion, but I hoped I got through to her. Her eyes fluttered; I could see the envelope.

My vision focused on it.

It was a bill. There was her address, visible through the clear plastic window set in the center of the envelope. I read it, my heart surging hope through me:

Britney Russell

713 N. Holland Way

That was it! I could tell the police where she was. I could save her life. I just had to get away. Had to escape from this rapture. I needed to wake up, but it felt so good. Dean's tongue licked at my clit, caressing it. He drowned me in rapture. Sparks of pleasure burst every time he caressed my bud. I groaned, squeezing my thighs around his head, my hands gripping his hair.

"I'm going to drown you in cream!" I howled, my orgasm swelling and swelling.

I had to get away. I had to wake up. This was a dream. A dream! I had to wake up. I needed to get back to my own body.

The ecstasy grew, my pussy squeezing as his tongue jammed into me. His digits stroked my clit, massaging it. The pressure of his rough fingertip teased me. He gave me the rapture that I craved, my orgasm building towards the ecstasy. My thighs quivered, opening wider as he feasted on me.

Two of his calloused fingers thrust into my cunt.

I came. Waves of bliss washed through my mind.

Wake up! I screamed at Britney.

The bliss drowned my thoughts, smothering them. Stars burst across my vision as I gasped out in wordless pleasure.

How could I wake up? This was just a dream!

The rapture took me higher and higher; I gasped and bucked and heaved and—

My eyes shot open. Shadow stood before me on my pillow, her green eyes inches from my face. I gasped in shock, flinching back in surprise. My body landed on the edge of my bed. I cried out as I fell off, yanking down my blanket with me. I landed on my side, my right hip throbbing.

I didn't care.

Where was my phone?

I fought to escape the tangled sheets, kicking my legs, squirming as I twisted my body around. I lifted myself by grabbing my nightstand for support. My phone was there, plugged into the charger. I grabbed it, turning it on. My fingers fumbled across the touchscreen. I had to call someone. I had to call...

911!

My phone rang and rang and rang. My stomach clenched. They had to pick up. Brittney was in danger.

"911, what is the nature of your emergency?" the cool, almost disinterested voice of the female operator answered.

"She's going to die!" I screamed into the phone. "You have to help her!"

~~*~~

An hour later, I was sitting on the couch in my living room, trembling. There was a police officer standing by the door, the cop who was parked out front of my apartment building to watch over me. Shadow was sprawled across my lap, purring as I nervously petted her. She was so warm, so alive.

"Still nothing?" I asked the cop.

"Sorry," he said. "They're at the scene, but I don't know exactly what's going on."

I swallowed, my fingers stroking over Shadow's silky fur. She purred, the rumble filling my soul. I was so glad I had her. Fear twisted at my stomach. What if I hadn't woken up in time?

A loud banging on my door made me jump.

"Open up!" a gruff voice growled. "It's Miller!"

The cop opened my door. The grizzled detective swept in, accompanied by his exhausted partner. Detective Jones had bags beneath her dark eyes. He, however, looked alert, almost manic as he marched towards me and growled, "How did you know?"

"Is she alive?" I asked, staring at him." Was I in time?"

He shook his head. "He didn't kill her the same way as the other two. It looked like he snapped her neck when we burst in. I think we interrupted him. My men saw him fleeing naked out the window, but they lost him in the dark. But we got every unit in the city crawling through the neighborhood. He won't be able to evade us long naked."

My stomach sank. "It was really him? Dean?"

"How did you know he was there?" Detective Miller asked, his eyes boring down on me.

"I..." I said. I blurted out the first thing that popped into my head: "He sent me a text. He told me where he was. Who he was with. I just... I was so afraid he might kill her, I had to make sure and..." My stomach sank. Dean really was a killer. He was just like Tyrone, a monster. I thought I could trust Dean, that he was different. The other night, after he kissed me, I would have let Dean inside my apartment even knowing he might be a killer.

If the cop hadn't driven by...

"I called you as soon as I could," I said, the tears coming, the back of my throat burning as my shoulders began to shake. "I wanted to save her. I tried."

Detective Jones sat down on the couch beside me, her arms slipping around my shoulders. She pulled me closer while Shadow purred louder. "I know you did," she said, her voice gentle. "It's okay. You did your best. It's not your fault that he's a monster."

"What does is it say about me that I'm attracted to monsters?" I asked, clutching to her. Shadow rubbed her whiskered face into my belly, trying to comfort me.

"We'll need your phone," Detective Miller said, his voice not as harsh as last time.

I stiffened. Dean *hadn't* texted me. What could I say now? I didn't know what to do. They'd never believe I had a dream. "It's in my bedroom."

Detective Miller strode across my living room and vanished down the hallway. I kept trembling in Detective Jones's embrace, her hand squeezing my shoulder. I petted Shadow without thought, my mind whirling. What would Miller say when he saw that there was no text message? What could I say that they would believe?

They would think I was crazy if I told them I had a dream. *I* thought I was crazy. Except...

"It's not your fault," Detective Jones said, her voice soft. "You didn't kill them. And it's not even your fault that you're attracted to him. That's what these sort of monsters do to people. Sociopaths are liars. Chameleons. They know exactly how to manipulate people. To make us think they're good because that's what we all want to think. Right? We all yearn for connections with others, to trust them. I know it doesn't really help, but you can't blame yourself. If you hadn't called 911, she would have suffered even worse things."

It didn't help.

"I don't see any message on your phone from him since the ones you told us about," Detective Miller growled as he re-entered the living room a moment later. "Nothing about him visiting the victim or anything."

"I don't know how that's possible," I lied, too scared to admit the truth. I couldn't stop myself now. "They came through. Honest." I shouldn't be deceiving them. They were cops. But... I couldn't think. Dean really killed that girl.

How could he be such a monster? He acted like he loved them. Like he worshiped them. When he was with me...

Fresh tears poured down my cheeks. I felt so dirty all of a sudden. So used. This was turning into such a nightmare. Why would he hurt those girls? What was wrong with him?

"Well, Kyrie?" Detective Miller demanded. "How did you know?"

"Maybe... maybe he hacked my phone," I said. "Maybe he deleted it? I don't know. It was there, so I called 911 to save the girl. Are you saying I'm working with him?" I shuddered. "I almost *became* one of those women."

He studied me, his face intent.

"Detective," the cop who was still standing by the door said. "They think they've spotted him by Meeker Park."

Detective Miller scrutinized me. "I'm taking your phone into evidence and handing it over to the technician. *Maybe* your phone was hacked."

I shuddered. I could feel the threat, but I didn't know what else to say. I just nodded.

"It's going to be fine," Detective Jones said, giving me another squeeze. "We're going to find him. He'll be stopped. Okay?"

I nodded my head.

"Why don't you go lie down. Officer Morgan will keep watching your apartment."

"I will," the cop said. "Right outside."

"We got him at Meeker Park," Jones said. "This will be over by the time you wake up in the morning."

I nodded again.

I clutched Shadow to my breasts as Detective Jones led me down the hallway to my bedroom. I stumbled after her, almost somnambulant. I was so dazed, exhausted by everything that had happened. I sank down on my bed, Shadow purring away. I stroked my cheek against her whiskers, her hot, rough tongue licking at my tears. Detective Jones gave me a smile before she closed the door behind her.

I stroked Shadow while all I could remember was poor Britney crying out in delight. She thought she was the luckiest woman in the world that Dean had visited her.

What a bastard! A goddamned monster! I couldn't believe I ever felt anything for him. That I was starting to... to... I didn't even want to admit what was happening. It made me feel dirty.

I wanted to take a shower.

Needed to take a shower.

The action galvanized me. Shadow hissed out in shock as I bolted upright, forcing her to leap free of my lap. She gave me a look.

I flushed, muttering, "Sorry."

I hurried out of my bedroom. Before showering, I double-checked that the deadbolt was locked. Then I set the chain, too. There was no way anyone could get in.

I headed towards the bathroom.

I stripped off my shirt and panties as the shower hissed. Naked, I hopped into the warm spray. I let it fall over me, washing Dean away from me. My body remembered his touch, the heat of his passion. I buried my face into the hot water, my red hair matted down until it clung to me. I braced my hands on the wall before me, my body shaking.

All these emotions swelled through me.

Grief for those poor women whose lives Dean stole. Such anger at him for hurting them. For tricking me. He was disgusting. Evil. I screamed out in rage, letting the impotence burst out of me. The spray rained on my face, warm caresses that washed over me as my anger spilled out of me.

Would I ever be clean?

The water grew cold. I turned the shower off and stumbled out of it. I dried myself mechanically, feeling that numbness sinking in again. I pulled on my shirt and panties and left my bathroom. I took two steps down the hallway towards my bedroom door and...

"Kyrie," his deep voice rumbled.

My gaze shot up. My breath caught in my throat. Dean stood at the entrance to the hallway, the light from my living room framing around his body. It made him almost seem like living darkness, a hole cut in reality. My stomach clenched at the sight of him. Somehow, there was a gleam in his blue eyes, reflecting light that didn't fall on his face.

Purring, Shadow rubbed against my naked feet. Her whiskers caressed me as she moved around me, sounding so happy. Reassuring. She didn't sense any danger at all while my heart pounded faster and faster. Dean, his hands out to his side like last night, took a step towards me.

"I'm not here to hurt you, Kyrie," he said. "We just need to talk. I need to explain things."

My stomach clenched.

"We need to understand—" he started to say, but fear launched me into action. I darted into my bedroom, throwing the door closed behind me.

CRASH!

I screamed for help as I rushed for my nightstand. I snagged the drawer's brass handle and wrenched it open. Clutter rattled around, including the .380 that I bought after Tyrone. I seized the pistol in trembling hands. Once a week, I went to the shooting range. I trained myself.

My thumb pressed down on the safety.

My bedroom door banged open.

"Kyrie, please, you don't need to be afraid. You're my devilish muse."

"Don't call me that!" I shrieked as I whirled around.

The gun felt so comfortable in my grip. It was a small pistol, perfectly sized for my dainty hand. I thrust my finger through the trigger guard. You only did that if you were prepared to shoot. I sighted down the weapon at him.

"I'm never going to be your victim!"

I pictured Tyrone standing there, his face thunderous rage.

I pulled the trigger.

Chapter Eight: Envy

The gun cracked as I pulled the trigger as fast as I could. The loud bangs assaulted my ears. Bright light flashed from the muzzle of the pistol. Bullets hurtled at Dean while I screamed with each shot, a primal release bursting from my soul.

I would not be a victim.

Dean threw himself to the hallway floor, diving out of sight while Shadow hissed in fear. I kept pulling the trigger, tracking him as he lunged for cover. Drywall burst in puffs of smoke as bullets slammed into the wall.

Click! Click! Click!

The gun dry fired. Empty. The slide was locked back, and nine shell casings were strewn across the floor and the comforter on my bed. A wisp of smoke curled from the barrel, a blue-gray haze in the air. The acrid stink stung my nose. My heart hammered in my chest.

Did I kill him?

I studied him lying in my hallway, his legs in view, the rest hidden. Dean's booted feet twitched.

I wasn't about to make the mistake of staying to find out. I turned around as I heard him groan. I darted towards my bedroom window and wrenched it open with a loud clatter. I yanked the screen out of the way and hurtled it down to the grass two stories below. It landed with a crash, the frame warping.

I swallowed at the drop. I had no choice. I could hear Dean

standing up in the background.

"Kyrie," he growled. "Wait, Kyrie."

No fear. I couldn't let terror hold me back. I stayed with Tyrone for so long because of it. First, because I was afraid to be a failure. I never made mistakes. I took pride in everything, including my relationships. Then I was just afraid that he would hurt me if I tried to leave him.

I wouldn't let that terror control me again. I was my own woman. I made my own decisions. I had made an amazing life for myself here, and no one was taking that away from me.

Pride swelling in me, I hurtled out the window.

My nightshirt fluttered around my thighs as the air whistled past me. The green grass, illuminated by the black lights of the apartment complex, rushed up at me. I hit the ground, knees flexing to absorb the impact.

I sprang into a sprint, shocked the landing didn't hurt.

"Kyrie, wait!" Dean roared above me.

I raced to the corner of the building. Officer Morgan was out front. He had to have heard the gunshots. I darted around the corner of the building, running at full sprint for the street. I had such energy, adrenaline pumping through my veins. I flowed, racing as I had in high school, arms pumping, legs stretching out before me. I was a championship runner again. I covered the distance in a flash, bursting around the building to rush past the courtyard.

I saw Officer Morgan crossing the road, his gun out. His eyes fell on me.

"It's him!" I screamed, pointing behind me.

I rushed for the cop as he grabbed his lapel microphone, speaking into it. His words were all nonsense to me, my heart pumping too much thunderous blood through my veins to hear anything else but my breathing. I reached him, his free hand thrusting me behind him. He aimed his gun in the direction I'd come while speaking into his radio at the same time.

In the distance, new sirens screamed to life; help incoming. I trembled, waiting for Dean to appear around the corner like a monster in a slasher film, barreling after me, unafraid of any cops. Whatever else he was, Dean wasn't a coward.

I was breathless, trembling, my fingers gripping the dark-blue cloth of the cop's uniform.

Dean never appeared.

Down the street, red and blue lights flashed. The first backup hurtling down the early morning street. There was no traffic on the street this early. The cop car raced closer and closer while more welcoming sirens filled the predawn air.

I let out a sigh of relief. I'd escaped him. I shuddered, pressing my face into the cop's back while tears fell down my cheeks.

Dean really was the killer. I was so wrong. I was so lucky to get away.

~~*~~

This night would never end. I had another round of talking to Detectives Miller and Jones. They were at a loss to explain how Dean could've crossed the city so fast. They were sure he was in the park. *Naked.* I begged them to let me go someplace safe. They agreed to take me to my friend Cyndi's place, promising that there would be a cop inside the room with me.

Officer Morgan volunteered.

The sun was just peeking over the horizon when we reached Cyndi's. She opened the door, her blue eyes raw-red and blurry. She wore a tight tank top that molded to her large breasts, her nipples pressing at the thin material. She looked different without her glasses on, younger, though her face was just as beautiful.

"Kyrie?" she gasped at the sight of me and Officer Morgan. "What's going on?" There was a breathlessness to her. I could see the fear fluttering through her body.

"Dean came for me," I gasped, throwing myself at her. I hugged her tight, clinging to my only friend.

"Dean?" she asked, confused. "What? Where? At your home?"

"I fought him off," I said. I held her so tight, squeezing my friend with all my passion. "Then I got away from him."

"She unloaded an entire .380 at him," Officer Morgan said. I felt a surge of pride at the praise in his words. "Then she jumped out of her window. I don't know how she didn't hurt herself."

"Used to compete in Track and Field in school," I said, my spine stiffening as I remembered all the medals I'd won. "I ran like I was in the 100m dash."

I felt giddy now. So alive all of a sudden. I had escaped. I clung to my friend, pulling her tight as life burst through me. I'd done it. I'd survived.

"What about Dean?" Cyndi asked. "I thought he would have fled or been caught by now or something."

"He's on the run now," said the cop, "which is why I'm going to be hanging out in your living room. If that's okay with you, miss?"

A throaty purr rumbled from Cyndi. "Well, that's more than fine. I've always been... *friendly* to the boys in blue."

"Cyndi!" I gasped. "This isn't the time to flirt."

She just laughed, hugging me tighter. "Let me get her settled down in my bedroom, then I'll make you some coffee. I bet you've been up all night Officer... um?"

"Morgan," he said. "Thank you. Two sugars, if you don't mind."

"You got it," she purred, then drew me through her living room to her hallway.

The giddiness bubbling through me continued as my friend led me down the hallway to her bedroom. The door was open, her bed neatly made. There was clothing scattered across the floor; delicate panties and sheer tops and flirty skirts were strewn carelessly about. I stepped carefully to avoid crushing any dainty things on the way to her bed.

I sat down on it, the mattress soft beneath my rump. I took a deep breath, trying to master my emotions. What was up with this almost drunk euphoria bubbling through me? Cyndi's fingers were feeling warm as she stroked my hand. She smiled, warm and supportive.

"Okay, let me make some coffee for that cute cop, then me and you will talk or do whatever you need." She winked a hazel eye at me.

"Thank you, Cyndi," I said, my body trembling. "It doesn't feel like anything's real right now."

"I bet," Cyndi said. Her hazel eyes narrowed. "He really came to your apartment?"

I nodded my head. "The police aren't sure how he evaded them. They were chasing him, naked, on the other side of town. He must have found a stash of clothes or something."

"Like he knew he would be running naked?" she asked. "Clever of him."

I shrugged my shoulders. I kicked my legs, dangling off the side of her bed, out before me. I wanted to run around. I had all this pent-up energy in me now. It was really hitting me that I had survived. I lived.

I didn't let Dean hurt me.

Cyndi closed the door behind her. I fell back on her bed, red hair spilling across the comforter. I listened to her as she padded down the hall, heard her bustling in the kitchen. My eyes flicked across the ceiling, studying the uneven shape of the rough, popcorn-like coating.

I hoped Shadow was all right. I had been so flustered, I didn't even think about my new cat. But she was independent. I doubt she'd have let that bastard hurt her. Besides, Dean was fixated on me.

It was like... he was trying to explain himself.

I was so panicked, I was so certain he was coming to hurt me, but... was he? He had approached me with his hands held low at his side. Maybe he was just trying to lull me into a false sense of security. I didn't wait to find out. I started firing at him before he could attack me. I might have even wounded him.

If he was injured, it would explain why he didn't chase after me.

I heard a murmuring conversation from the living room, then footsteps thudded down the hallway. The door opened. Cyndi slipped in. "Well, Officer Morgan is taken care of. I made him my best coffee."

I sat up and said, "If you want to go out there and flirt with him, I'm okay. Really."

"Of course not," Cyndi huffed. "I'd rather be right here with you." She flew to the bed, her large breasts bouncing in that tight tank top she wore.

Her nipples were hard.

She sank down beside me, her arms sweeping about my shoulders. She pulled me close to her like Detective Jones had. Only... Her fingers were so warm on my arm. I felt the swell of her right breast pressing against my left side. Her hazel eyes brewed with some strange passion. Her lips were red, shiny.

"There's no place I'd rather be than right here. I'm with my Kyrie."

My Kyrie?

She kissed me.

I went rigid, confused at the heat of her mouth on mine. Her tongue thrust past my lips. Her hand on my shoulder tightened while the other darted across her body to cup my round breasts through my nightshirt. She gave a light squeeze, just teasing me with her fingers as her tongue raced through my mouth.

Her lips tasted sweet, her hard nipple poking into the side of my left breast. My own nubs hardened in a flash. This heat swirled in me, feeding off my elation at surviving the attack. I couldn't help how my body reacted to this stimuli.

I struggled to think.

I knew Cyndi was bi, but I didn't think she had any feelings for me. I was gripped by the shock of the kiss, my mind reeling as her tongue fluttered through my mouth. She caressed my breast, teasing me as she kissed me with such passion. I groaned, trembling.

She tasted sweet.

Her fingers slid across my breast and found my hard nipple. She twisted and played with it, sending tingling delight shooting down to my pussy. My snatch grew hotter and hotter, soaking my panties. My toes curled against the soft bedroom carpet. The mattress creaked as she shifted, groaning into the kiss. She was pressing me backward. I should be resisting her, stopping her, but I let her push me down onto her bed.

My red hair spread across her comforter, my body trembling. She broke the kiss, her hazel eyes glossy with passion. She stared down at me, her cheeks flushed. "Oh, Kyrie, I've wanted this for so long. I've wanted you so badly. You're so sexy. You're like me, aren't you? You have that bit of darkness in you."

"What?"

She kissed me again, her tongue thrusting into my mouth while she worked my nipple through my nightshirt. My entire body shuddered. If it wasn't for the crazy events of tonight, I would be lost to this passion. But this wasn't right. She shouldn't be doing this right now. This was the wrong time. I couldn't trust my feelings right now. Not after all the shock I'd been through the last few days.

I had to slow this down.

I pushed on her shoulder, not hard, just to pry her lips away from mine. I needed to breathe. Think. But how could I with her wet lips working against mine and her tongue dancing around inside my mouth? She rolled my nipple through my nightshirt again. The tingles rushed to my pussy, causing my thighs to squeeze tight together, my clit throbbing, aching in need.

I pushed harder at her shoulder.

She broke away from me.

"Wait, wait, you're going too fast," I gasped. "Cyndi, I'm not into girls."

Except in dreams.

"Mmm, I know what you like," Cyndi purred.

She kissed me again, harder, with more aggression. Both my hands gripped her shoulders this time, squeezing and pushing back as her lips changed as they kissed me. They grew stronger, rougher. I

106

felt stubble rasping against my cheeks while beneath my fingers, muscles formed. She grew strong, solid, her torso broadening. Her hazel eyes became a deep, intense blue while her blonde hair transformed into a wild mane of black locks.

She became Dean.

My jaw dropped as I stared up into the face of Dean. Only moments ago, my friend Cyndi was kissing me, but now...

A shrill, hysterical giggle burst from my lips. I couldn't help it. I was going insane. My hands trembled as I reached up and stroked his strong jawline. I felt the stubbly whiskers of Dean. Not the soft, feminine features of my friend Cyndi. Her hazel eyes were gone. Her blonde hair was replaced with Dean's wild and shaggy mane of black locks. Her face was replaced with the brooding, handsome features that had first captured my attention when he walked into the club.

And those eyes... Those intense, blue eyes were his.

"What is going on?" I asked, my words breaking. "The dreams, and now this. Cyndi... I..."

"*This* is what you want, Kyrie," Dean said, his words thick with bitterness. "I became him. I can become anything that you want. You're just so beautiful." Dean stroked my cheek. His fingers rough yet tender. "You're my goddess, Kyrie. Ever since I first met you, I knew. You have that darkness in you. Just like me."

"Darkness?" I shuddered. "Dean, how are you here? What's happened to Cyndi?"

"I *am* Cyndi," he growled. His voice was so passionate. "I became him to love you. You inspired such passion in me, Kyrie. The moment I met you, you made me so wet.

"Now you make me so hard."

"Wet? Hard?" I asked. "You can't be Dean. I've seen you two together."

I was going insane. That was what was happening. Another burst of shrill laughter escaped my lips, my mind cracking under the strain. This didn't make any sense. I shuddered as his—her?—hand stroked down my cheek to my throat. Then his—or her?—lips found mine. She kissed me with such passion, thrusting her tongue into my mouth.

My body responded, remembering the intensity of being with Dean in the alley. In my dreams. This was such a wondrous delight. Her tongue dueled with mine, her hand stroking lower down my neck, reaching the hem of my nightshirt. She caressed downward to cup my breast through the cloth, rubbing my hard nipple. Tingles raced through me as I moaned into the kiss.

Cyndi-Dean broke the kiss, groaning, "My beautiful, dark goddess."

Goddess... Just like in the dreams. "You're really Cyndi?" I asked. "I mean...?"

For a moment, Cyndi's hazel eyes peered down at me from Dean's face. Then they were all blue again. "I can be whoever you need me to be, Kyrie. Just let me worship you. You're so perfect. Not like the others."

"Others...?"

Cyndi-Dean kissed down to my neck, nibbling at my flesh. Lips rough and strong, the stubble rasping against my sensitive flesh. My toes curled as tingles raced through me. My pussy grew hotter and hotter as I struggled to think. What did she mean by others?

My stomach clenched as realization crystallized inside of me.

"Did you...?" I didn't want to ask. I didn't want to find out that my friend was a... "Did you kill those women?"

"When you told me about your dreams," moaned Cyndi-Dean, those piercing, blue eyes staring down at me. Her hand squeezed my breasts harder. "I was so delighted that it had worked. That you had witnessed it. You knew exactly what I did to those women. How I worshiped their bodies. How I loved them. But it wasn't *me* they wanted.

"It was him!" Bitterness twisted Cyndi-Dean's rugged features, making her look vile. Disgusting. "When I revealed my true form to them, they always screamed. They didn't want me. I worshiped them, gave them what they craved, but they refused to give me what I NEEDED!"

Icy hands squeezed my stomach, another gripping my heart.

108

The rage that crossed Cyndi-Dean's face was so familiar. I'd seen it on Tyrone's. That wrath. That passionate anger. It was a darkness that had to lash out and hurt something.

"You did it!" I gasped. "You killed them!"

"I took such joy in it. After they rejected me, they deserved to pay!" Cyndi-Dean shuddered. "I just wanted to worship them. To love them. Why couldn't they love me back?" Her hand slid up from my breast to caress my cheek.

I wanted to flinch. It felt just like Dean's masculine touch.

"You're not going to reject me, right, Kyrie?" she asked, her voice softening. "You're my friend. You care for me."

Panic flooded through me. "Officer Morgan!" I howled. "Officer Morgan, help, help!"

At the same moment, my legs flashed up, planting right between Cyndi-Dean's legs. Right against her balls. Pain flashed across her face, blue eyes bulging for a moment. I squirmed, thrusting with both my arms against her muscled chest, pushing away my mad friend.

I wiggled out from beneath her, rolling across the bed and gaining my feet. "Officer Morgan!" I shouted as I rushed for the door. "Please, please, help!"

I seized the doorknob and twisted.

A powerful, iron-strong hand grabbed the back of my neck. I screamed as Cyndi-Dean threw me down to the bedroom floor. Air burst from my lungs while pain flared across my rump. She stood over me, her muscular chest rippling with passion. She had such a hateful look twisting those handsome features. Madness glowed in her blue eyes.

"Even you?" Cyndi-Dean roared.

I scrabbled backward from Cyndi-Dean, my heart thundering in my chest. Fear pumped through my veins, my blood burning with liquid fright. My head cast around, my red locks flying as I searched for a way to escape. But my transformed friend was between me and the door, a hulking presence.

"Even you reject me!" she roared, advancing with heavy steps; a hard cock thrust rampant before her.

"You killed those women!" I gasped, gaining my feet, pain flaring across my rump as my bruised muscles flexed. I needed a weapon. "You murdered them because they weren't into girls? Because they were into Dean and not you?"

"Yes!" hissed Cyndi-Dean. It sounded so feminine coming from such masculine lips. For a moment, Cyndi's hazel eyes peered at me. "I searched and searched for a woman to accept *me!*" Her eyes glared at me. "That was supposed to be you, Kyrie! But even you reject me!"

"Of course I fucking reject you!" I snarled, head whipping around. I spotted her heavy bedside lamp. I snatched the porcelain body, fingers clenching around the mauve ceramic. I yanked hard, ripping the cord out of the wall socket. "You're a murderer! Officer Morgan, help!"

She laughed, a deep, rumbling sound. "Officer Morgan can't help anyone. He's dying in the living room. I brewed him my *special* coffee."

A cold shiver ran down my spine, fear's touch caressing me. How had I missed that this evil thing was inside Cyndi? "You're disgusting! You're just as filthy and foul as Tyrone!"

I hurtled the lamp at Cyndi-Dean. She threw up a meaty arm, the ceramic shattering against her. Shards of porcelain spilled around her, the lamp's core bouncing off her arm and hitting the ground. The light bulb shattered, spilling more sharp glass across the floor. Small cuts bled across her arm, crimson ribbons dribbling across her tan skin. Corded muscles rippled across her chest as Cyndi-Dean roared in fury.

"Don't pretend you don't love what I've done," she growled, marching forward. Cyndi-Dean stepped on a piece of a broken lamp, the ceramic cracking beneath her step. She didn't flinch even as she left behind a bloody footprint. "You're just like me. I can see that shadow in you. You inhabited those women. You stole their pleasure and made it your own. You felt everything I gave them."

"I'm nothing like you, bitch!" I snarled, backing up until I bumped into the nightstand. My fingers scrambled across the smooth, polished surface of the nightstand, searching for a weapon.

I brushed her alarm clock.

I yanked hard, ripping its plug from the socket. I hurtled it at her face. It crashed into Cyndi-Dean's brow, the plastic body bouncing off and striking the ceiling before clattering to the floor behind her.

Cyndi-Dean stepped closer.

"I'll show you that darkness in you," growled my twisted friend. With a blur, her cut arm shot out at me. Her thick hand seized my neck, iron-strong fingers crushing my throat.

My scream choked off as my trachea cracked. I thrashed, my fingernails clawing at the rock-hard muscles of her forearm. I scratched as she squeezed the life out of me. Cyndi-Dean slammed me backward, sliding my rump over her nightstand, and drove me into the wall. I would have grunted if I could. The drywall cracked behind me. Pain radiated up and down my spine. She loomed over me, those piercing, blue eyes boiling with rage.

"When I take you apart, I'll show you that darkness inside of you!" Cyndi-Dean growled. "As you're screaming, begging me to forgive you, I'll show you what a monster you are, Kyrie! You! Are! Just! Like! *ME!*"

Spots of darkness danced around my vision. My heart pounded; my head swelled with the pressure of the trapped blood. My lungs burned. I needed to breathe. More and more of the shadows swallowed my world, my gaze narrowing until Cyndi-Dean's maddened face filled my vision. I beat futile fists against her broad chest.

I had to breathe.

A primal, animal panic swelled through me. I didn't want to die. I grew weaker and weaker and...

A second Dean appeared.

Strong hands went around Cyndi-Dean's throat.

The real Dean wrenched back the impostor from me and he hurled my monstrous friend to the ground.

Chapter Nine: The Changeling's Envy

Kyrie Hope

I drew in a ragged breath then coughed, my throat burning. I shuddered, struggling to speak as the real Dean stood before me, dressed in that black leather jacket, his red t-shirt stretched over his brawny chest. He had blood caked on his cheek from a long, narrow wound.

I must have grazed him with a shot earlier.

"You okay?" growled the real Dean.

I struggled to speak, but I could only cough. So I nodded.

His hands balled into fists as he rounded on the fake. Cyndi-Dean scrambled to her feet, stepping back onto the shattered lamp. My friend swelled larger. I could hear the creak of bones enlarging, the rasp of sinew rubbing on sinew. She grew more and more muscular, veins bulging against naked skin. With a mad rage, Cyndi-Dean threw a blurring punch, the air roaring around her blow.

The real Dean ducked, flowing like shadows. His own fist slammed into the fake's side. Cyndi-Dean grunted, annoyance flickering across her face. With a growl, my mad friend brought both her fists together, forming them into a crushing ball that she raised over her head. Howling, she slammed her combined hands down at the real Dean's back.

"Look out!" I croaked through a bruised throat.

~~*~~

Dean Walker

Death hurtled down at me, a meteor plunging at my body. I dodged to the right as the blow hurtled past me. The air of its passage washed over me. The doubled-up fists crashed into the bedroom floor. The concrete slab beneath the carpet shook. A sharp crack echoed through the room.

How strong could she become?

The changeling grew more ropy muscles. I could hear its flesh groaning as it added more sinew and swelled the size of her bones. More strands of bulging might swelled up its limbs, its head—*my* head!—brushing the ceiling.

"YOU BASTARD!" howled the changeling in my own voice. "THEY ALL WANTED *YOU!*"

"Gehenna's burning depths!" I snarled as I drew my thick knife from beneath my jacket.

The long blade of my knife did little to give the changeling pause. Its eyes—*my* eyes—flicked down at the blade for a moment. The razor-sharp edge, tapering towards a sharp point, gleamed. It was military issue, a weapon of war.

Did the changeling even feel pain right now? Had it modified its body that much? Was that why it didn't care about my weapon? It was stepping barefoot on the broken ceramic scattered across the carpet and was bleeding from numerous cuts on its forearm.

Kyrie scrambled over the bed as the hulking version of myself drew back its fist. I dodged the barreling punch. It screamed past my head. I ducked a second blow, a wild haymaker thrown from the left. I felt its passage scream over my head as I plunged the knife at

113

the changeling's muscular abs.

A powerful knee thrust up and slammed into my arm, throwing off my attack, the blade stabbing past the changeling. I threw myself back, sensing an incoming attack. I hurtled clear as its massive elbow crashed down where I had been standing.

It would have crushed my skull.

Ceramic shattered beneath my boots as I shifted my stance, drawing the knife back, ready to thrust or slash. The hulk followed as I backed away, snarling in rage. I could see the envy burning in its blue eyes as it punched hard at me.

"THEY ALL WANTED YOU!" boomed the monstrosity.

I dodged.

"NOT ME! THEY WANTED YOUR CHISELED JAW!"

I hit the wall, narrowly avoiding another blow.

"THEY ALL WANTED YOUR BRAWNY PHYSIQUE!"

I dropped down. Her fist slammed into the wall above me. Drywall rained across my back. I dove to my left, rolling clear of a lashing foot. My leather jacket rasped over shards of broken pottery. I came up in a crouch.

"THEY DIDN'T WANT MY LUSH BREASTS!" it howled.

Its foot slammed down and almost crushed me. Concrete snapped. The entire building shook.

"Dean!" Kyrie screamed, backed into the corner of the room by a dark-stained dresser. Her green eyes caught mine, shining with fear. I had to protect her.

I had to defend my devilish muse. No woman had inspired me as much as Kyrie did since the angel, and...

I shoved down the pain. Now wasn't the time to dwell on old wounds.

"NONE OF THEM WANTED TO EAT MY PUSSY!" howled the envious changeling.

Its fist hurled at me. I ducked low and stabbed.

My blade scored across rippling abs, slashing through hard flesh. Blood spilled down in a crimson sheet towards its thighs and groin. I slashed again, leaving another wound slicing diagonally up its chest. Then I darted back, avoiding a powerful right cross.

I hit the wall behind me.

"Dean!" shrieked Kyrie.

I realized in a flash that I'd made a mistake by dodging this direction. I had the wall behind me, the hulk before me. I had to be precise with my next move. I'd get one chance to escape. I tensed, waiting for its attack to come.

With a bellow, the changeling's fist crashed down at my head. The barreling blow that would crush my skull if it connected. I ducked low and—

It anticipated this escape.

Its knee flashed up at me and crashed into my chest. Ribs snapped. The blow threw me back. Air exploded from my lungs as I slammed into the wall. It shattered behind me. I kept flying, debris raining around me. I landed on the kitchen floor, my body twitching from the pain. I coughed up blood, the knife spilling from my spasming fingers.

"No, no, Dean!" Kyrie screamed in terror.

~~*~~

Kyrie Hope

Cyndi-Dean turned around; the transformed hulk was bleeding but didn't seem to care about its wounds. Crimson covered its lower torso and spilled down its right thigh. She stared at me with such rage. Her lips peeled back, showing teeth grown sharp, turned into snarling fangs.

Shark fangs.

I cowered against the wall. What could I do against her? She had just killed Dean. I didn't know what to do.

Cyndi-Dean grabbed her bed and hurled it to the side. It slammed into her closet door, bed frame snapping, mattress tumbling to the floor, spilling sheets and pillows everywhere. The room shook as my hulking friend advanced on me.

"THIS IS WHAT YOU WANT!" snarled Cyndi-Dean. She grabbed her dick swollen to such immense size. It was a cock that wouldn't give pleasure.

Only pain.

"YOU WANTED THIS FUCKING DICK! SO YOU CAN LOVE IT!" she thundered. "YOU CAN SQUEAL ON MY FUCKING COCK, BITCH!"

I was dead. She was too fast. Too huge. She loomed between me and the door. I couldn't get away. I whimpered as death advanced.

Green eyes flashed. A dark shape blurred across the floor, darting from the door and around my monstrous friend. The thing was small and fast. It leaped at me, landing in my arms. I blinked at the warm, furry body clutched to my breasts. It purred, a sound of hope and confidence.

Shadow stared up at me with her loving, green eyes.

I clutched my new cat, trembling as her warmth bled through me. Her purr was stirring. She was trying to comfort me. She had no idea that there was no escape. That there was nothing that she could do to save me and...

She became shadows.

My cat melted around me, engulfing me in the fuzzy warmth of darkness. My body moved, animated by the umbral aura about me. I darted away, gasping in shock as Cyndi-Dean suddenly slowed. She reached out to grab me, but her thick fingers moved like a glacier. They covered inches while I covered feet. I was racing past her, moving with the darkness around me.

Just like Dean would when he'd appear out of the shadows.

I darted past Cyndi-Dean's outstretched fingers, a slow, rumbling growl bursting from the monstrous hulk's lips. I moved so fast it was easy to avoid her grab. I danced over the mattress and spilled blankets with grace. I navigated the rubble from Dean smashing through the wall without tripping, my bare feet landing on the carpet with all the dexterity of a cat.

I burst into the hallway, the shadows along the wall reaching for me. They wanted to embrace me, take me away.

We have to go, Shadow whispered in my soul, her voice a feminine purr. I knew that voice from the dream. *Can you feel my essence wanting to merge with the darkness around us?*

I did.

"What about Dean?" I asked, bursting into the living room. Officer Morgan lay prone on the ground, his fingers bent in horrible ways, foam staining his lips. In the kitchen, Dean was on his back, blood coating his lips, his body splayed, bent. "Is he dead?"

My owner wants you safe! shouted Shadow in my mind. *Kyrie, flow into the darkness. Hurry. I can't keep you moving faster for much longer. He wants you protected! You've touched his soul. His heart! Please, Kyrie, flee!*

Reality lurched around me. The deep, rumbling growl of Cyndi-Dean crashed into me at its normal rate, becoming audible words, "GET BACK HERE! YOU ARE *MINE!*"

You have to flee now, or she'll kill you! Shadow begged. Her dark aura around me quivered. The umbral pools reaching across the carpet, the absences of light scattered around the living room, called to me. I could step into them. Flee.

"Dean!" I screamed. "I'm sorry I didn't trust you!" Tears fell down my cheeks as Cyndi-Dean crashed through her bedroom doorway, shattering wood and drywall. She filled the hallway, an immensity of wrath. "I should have trusted my heart, Dean! I'm sorry! I was confused! You warned me about lies!"

"GET OVER HERE, CUNT!" bellowed Cyndi-Dean, her monstrous, elephantine cock thrusting out towards me.

Dean shuddered. His hands curled. He coughed up blood as he rose. His blue eyes met mine.

"I understand," he growled. "Go!"

Somehow, this amazing man lived. He moved. Stood. He snatched up his long-bladed knife stained with Cyndi-Dean's blood.

I stepped towards the reaching shadows and let the darkness embrace me.

~~*~~

Dean Walker

Everything hurt.

The hulking changeling barreled into the living room, reaching for the shadows where Kyrie had vanished. Elizabeth took Kyrie away, my familiar obeying my commands. She was a loyal creature, her essence bonded to mine. I knew Elizabeth would rather stay and help me fight. Not because if I died she would melt back into the torment of Gehenna, but because she loved me.

But I had to protect Kyrie. She was more important than my soul.

"WHERE DID SHE GO!" howled the changeling as she whirled around to face me.

How could I hurt the monstrosity? It was so huge. I glanced down at my five-inch blade. Was it big enough to hurt her? The changeling had increased its mass so much, its envy driving it to be something more than it ever was. The changeling was like me, like Kyrie, a half-devil.

A cambion.

Only the changeling had given into its darkness. The thing had cast its lot with its infernal heritage, its devilish essence twisting its humanity. The changeling had murdered. It had used its power to perpetrate evil and was lost to the sin of its existence.

I would've fallen down the same trap if it wasn't for her... My sweet angel.

The pain in my heart swelled over the agony of my battered body. I'd lost my angel, but now I had Kyrie to protect.

I grit my teeth. I would have to kill the changeling to protect Kyrie. I had to plunge my weapon into its chest. Its heart. A single thrust that would deliver a mortal blow. There was no other way. I couldn't endure more injuries.

I hurt, but I rushed forward.

The changeling bellowed, drawing back its arm, knuckles crackling as it clenched its hand into a ball the size of my head. With a loud bellow, she punched a huge fist at me, delivering death.

I didn't dodge or duck the blow.

I leaped over it.

My body wasn't human. My mother was a devil from the bowels of hell, and her infernal blood flowed through me. She gave me my incubal hungers. She made me handsome and irresistible to women. She gave me the strength and toughness that dedicated me to one goal...

Pleasing women.

Kyrie.

A look of shock crossed the changeling's face as I soared over its fist, my knife plunging straight at its heart. I hurtled too fast for it to do anything about my attack. No dodging or blocking. My blade slammed into its chest, burying to the hilt. The knife slipped past ribs to find its heart.

I slammed into its brawny chest and rebounded. I lost my grip on my knife. I crashed to the floor at its feet. The changeling roared in pain, the knife buried deep. Blood welled around the hilt, spilling down its muscular chest. It swayed. I expected it to fall over, its heart ruined, no longer pumping life to sustain it.

That killed even one of us.

"THIS IS THE BEST YOU CAN DO?" it bellowed, blood coating its lips. It ripped my blade from its chest, blood gushing out. The entire knife was coated in its life. It should be dead, but...

I groaned as I I realized my miscalculation. The changeling had grown so brawny, so huge, that the blade wasn't long enough to reach its heart. I didn't deliver that immediately fatal wound. It might die in the next ten minutes, but I wouldn't last that long.

It laughed louder, bloody spittle flying from its lips as it crushed the knife in its broad hand, ruining the blade. It hurtled it to the ground and raised its foot to smash down on me.

As I rolled clear, I knew I needed to do something else. I needed another weapon.

The dying cop groaned.

The cop was dying, foam covering his lips. He twitched on the floor, fingers spasming with unnatural twitches. The changeling wanted the poor bastard out of the way while it enjoyed my Kyrie. My eyes fixed on the cop's utility belt.

On his sidearm.

I had one chance.

The changeling raised a mighty foot to crush me. I forced my battered body to spring away. I lunged toward the cop.

~~*~~

Kyrie Hope

I gasped as I stumbled out of the shadows, my hands gripping the familiar frame of my own bed. The darkness surrounding me bled away and formed not the cat version of Shadow, but into the woman from my dreams. That dusky-skinned beauty I saw dancing with Dean the first night I met him. She had the same green eyes as my cat, only they weren't slitted. She threw a look over her shoulder, biting her lower lip.

She was gazing in the direction of Cyndi's apartment.

"Is he dying?" I demanded. "Can we help him?"

"You can't help him," Shadow said, shaking her head, her mane of dark hair spilling about her shoulders.

"What about you?" I gasped. I grabbed her shoulders and spun her around. I stared into her green eyes. "You could've saved him like you did me. You can go back to him and transport him across the... the.. whatever it was we just did."

Then I saw the exertion filling her expression, the sheen of sweat across her creamy-brown features. "You are not... my master..." she panted, her naked breasts rising and falling. "It is... more difficult... to bring you through the darkness... than him."

I stared at her with such helpless desperation. "What about

120

Dean? How can he win?" Tears spilled down my cheeks. "I... I think..."

Shadow hugged me tight. She wasn't trying to comfort me, but clutched to me, trembling. "I know. I can look into your soul. But I'm still here. That means he's still alive. He's strong. He's a cambion. Like you."

"Cambion?"

~~*~~

Dean Walker

The changeling's foot slammed into the floor behind me. The entire apartment shook. Pictures hanging on the wall crashed to the ground, glass shattering. Agony screamed through me as I rolled across the carpet and ended in a crouch by the dying cop.

His eyes were rolled back in his head, his twitching slowing. I could do nothing about the poison. All I could do was kill the monster who'd hurt him. To stop this vile changeling from destroying any more lives. My hands seized the cop's hip, grabbing something cylindrical on his belt. With a grunt, I rolled him over so I could get access to his handgun. I ripped the 9mm out of its holster.

A crushing grip seized my arm. Squeezed.

My bones fractured.

I screamed and dropped the gun as the changeling wrenched me up into the air. I dangled from its grip, my hand brushing the ceiling. An evil grin crossed its face, shark-like fangs filling a hungry maw. The changeling was utterly gone, consumed by the taint of its dark heritage.

"Hellbound bitch!" I snarled.

An evil rumble burst from the changeling's fang-filled mouth. "I'll keep you alive. Let you watch as I fuck your precious Kyrie to death. She should have chosen *ME!*"

The changeling shook me, pain rippling down my arm and consuming my body. My broken ribs ground together. I coughed up more blood while my left hand clenched on something... cylindrical. I was holding something when she ripped me up from the cop. It had come free from the utility belt. I glanced down and saw I held a can of mace.

"I WOULD'VE LOVED HER!" growled the changeling, its deep voice shaking my battered body. "I WOULD HAVE WORSHIPED HER LIKE A GODDESS! I WOULD HAVE GIVEN HER SUCH RAPTURE! SHE JUST HAD TO ACCEPT ME AND EMBRACE THE DARKNESS INSIDE OF HER!"

I shoved the can of mace in its face and depressed the trigger. White foam burst from it, splattering across its face. Instantly, my eyes burned. The monstrous thing howled in rage, its mouth opening wide. I fired the sticky mace right down its gullet. The thing choked and growled, head shaking. I screamed as my broken arm wrenched, then it threw me to the floor. It stumbled back, clawing at its face to clean off the foam.

The world grew blurry. Tears spilled out of my burning eyes. I couldn't see anything. Everything was distorted. I had to find something. I cast my distorted gaze around and spotted it.

The discarded pistol.

My left arm lunged for it, my right screaming in agony as the broken bones ground together. I seized the pistol's grip. I raised it. Aimed.

"I WILL RIP YOU APART!" howled the changeling looming over me. "I WILL—"

I unloaded all the rounds in the weapon. The handgun barked as I pulled the trigger again and again and again. Bullets slammed into the blurry hulk. It roared, reeling back. I couldn't tell if I was hurting it.

I just kept pulling the trigger.

"YOU CAN'T HAVE HER!" it roared and lurched toward me.

It clawed at its face, bellowing and gurgling as it loomed over me. I tried to crawl backward, my broken body swimming in pain.

The gun clicked dry, every round spent.

I was dead.

I threw the useless weapon to the side and forced myself back again. The monstrous hulk reached for me, swayed. Then, with a gurgling growl, it pitched forward and crashed to the floor at my feet.

"She's... mine..." the changeling croaked, dying. "Miiiinneeee."

Through my blurry vision, I watched the figure change, its flesh flowing. It shrank, muscles melting away to reveal something slender, something dainty.

The pain surged through me. I groaned and collapsed. Darkness's cool embrace seized me, pulling me down... down...

Into...

My angel smiled at me.

Chapter Ten: Shadowy Passion Unleashed

Kyrie Hope

"Kyrie..." groaned Dean.

My eyes latched onto Dean. My heart exploded into a wild beast as I sat up in my chair. I grabbed his left hand, his right arm cradled in a makeshift sling that Elizabeth had made for him.

Not Shadow like I thought. The name of the cat-woman was Elizabeth.

"I'm here, Dean," I said, clutching his hand. Fresh tears spilled down my cheeks as relief flared through me. He was awake. "You did it. You saved me."

This giddy burst of delight shuddered through me. When Elizabeth had first appeared out of the shadows with Dean, after she recovered her metaphysical "breath" and had the strength to fetch him, I was shocked by the sight of the incubus. Horrified by how battered he was. His arm was mangled, his blood soaking his lips, his breathing wheezing out of him. I begged for him to go to the hospital, but Elizabeth refused.

"The darkness in him will heal him," she'd said with a bitter twist to her words.

Dean squeezed my hand back, his grip surprisingly strong

considering his condition a few hours ago. I sniffed, fighting against the emotion wanting to pour out of me. I didn't want to fall apart. I leaned over him, my red hair tumbling about my face, a few strands caressing my cheeks. I kissed him on the lips. His were so firm and strong, so powerful despite his wounds. Whiskers rasped against my sensitive skin. I could taste the faint hint of coppery blood.

A strange, dark exhilaration swirled through me. *You're my goddess, Kyrie. Ever since I first met you, I knew. You have that darkness in you. Just like me.*

I broke the kiss, trembling. "Are you really okay? I can still take you to a hospital. Elizabeth wouldn't let me, but..."

"I'll survive," he growled. His strong grip squeezed my hand again. "Not the first time I've been hurt this bad."

"No, it's not," Elizabeth said, the strange cat-woman looking down at her hands folded on her lap, her naked breasts jiggling. Was that... guilt making her squirm? What had she done?

"Where are we?" groaned Dean.

"At a safe house, I guess," I said, glancing around the one-room, basement apartment we were in. It was old but clean. It was so austere the TV, one of those old ones and not a flat screen, sat on the floor. Besides the bed, there was no other furniture. "We've been here for a while. Elizabeth brought us after she saw you were stabilized and before the police could come to check out my apartment."

"Police?" Dean asked. Then he groaned. "Right, right, the changeling killed one of them."

"What was my friend?" I gasped, the sudden swelling of pain rippling through me. "What is a changeling? I thought she was my friend... But she wanted to hurt me." The words Cyndi had said echoed through my mind. "How do I keep opening myself up to monsters?"

"Because you have a warm heart," Dean said, his thumb stroking the back of my hand. "You can only be betrayed when you open up your heart to those around you. When you allow your *humanity* to flourish. Cyndi..." He sighed. "She fell to the sin that pumps through our veins."

"Are you talking about that original sin, Catholic nonsense?" I asked, Cyndi's words still rippling through me. I couldn't be like her. I would never kill anyone.

Dean shook his head. "Cyndi was like me. Like you." His eyes stared at me. "She was a cambion. Half human, half devil."

I blinked at him. "What?" I shook my head. "Cambion? Elizabeth mentioned something about that."

"That's what we're called," Dean said. "Those of us who have an infernal parent. We come in different... flavors. We're based on the seven deadly sins. Cyndi was what is called a changeling. I'm an incubus." A surge of electricity rippled out of his touch, arcing through my body.

My nipples hardened. A molten heat swelled in between my thighs.

"I'm sure you felt that wild attraction to me. That lust to get naughty and writhe with me. You see how I am around women. They all want me."

I nodded, swallowing. "I mean you're just... handsome. A gorgeous, rugged man. That's..." My words faltered off. Was even a movie star fawned over as much as Dean was? Did every woman want to fuck Chris Hemsworth or Chris Evans or Justin Mamoa that much?

"My mother was a lust demon," continued Dean. "She called herself Ash. My father had a one-night stand with her, and she left me on his doorstep nine months later. I didn't meet her until... later."

I swallowed. My mother had a one-night stand, too. Did that mean...? "Still, I mean, devils? They're not real."

"Did you not see your friend transform?" asked Elizabeth. Her green eyes focused on mine, their emerald brilliance contrasting with the dusky hue of her face. "How do you explain how Dean was able to survive his injuries? Or the pleasure he gives women just by dancing with them." Her eyes narrowed. "How you are able to inhabit those women's dreams."

126

I swallowed.

"I can see it in your eyes," Dean said. "Who was your absentee parent? Your mother or your father?"

I swallowed. "My father. My mother had a one-night stand with him. She never forgot about him, but she only knew his name. Sterling."

"A fitting name for a pride demon," said Dean.

"Pride?" Then I swallowed. My cheeks flushed. I did like to take pride in my life. In being the best at my job, or making sure my apartment looked as good as I could make it. I took pride in my appearance, in my relationships. I always had.

"Pride cambion, called lilins, can enter into other people's minds. They can experience the world through them, judging themselves against the other person. Seeing if they are better than them or not. If they think they are, they can take control of the person."

I swallowed. Trembling. "And a changeling?"

"Envy cambion," Dean said. "That's what lets them change their form. They become the person they're most envious of."

Envy had definitely defined Cyndi. She was always jealous of other girls and their dresses. She was always talking about how she'd look better in their clothing than they would. I thought it was normal girl talk. "Was it envy that led her to... kill those girls?"

Dean nodded. "And they weren't her first, either." Dean winced and pain flashed across his face. His arm, the one in a sling, twitched. "Damn... I'm fine..." He drew in a deep breath. "Anyway, Elizabeth and I have been tracking her for a few weeks, following the trail of dead women and men that led to here. She moved to town not long after you did, right?"

I nodded my head. "I guess so. A few months back. Both of us being new gave us something to bond over."

"Well, she was part of some... machination of the Lords of Hell. And we found you in the middle of it. A cambion who'd never given in to her sin. I think Cyndi was trying to corrupt you. Once one of us gives in to the darkness, into our worst nature, we're lost. Become monsters."

I shuddered.

"So, what, Cyndi's responsible for me dreaming as those women?" I asked.

"Probably," Dean said. "I can't be sure, but Elizabeth detected something leading you to the last woman's dream."

I glanced at Elizabeth—it was hard not to think of her as Shadow—sitting on the other side of the bed. "You slipped into my dream and you... ate me out." My cheeks warmed. "Was that real?"

A smile crossed her lips. "Oh, you were only half dreaming for that. I really did eat you out. I just couldn't resist. You had my owner's cum in you. I do so love licking his jizz out of a woman." She shuddered, her tongue flicking across her lips. She said those words with such a breathy tone, full of passion.

Heat rippled from my pussy.

"And then you slipped into another dream," Elizabeth continued, "and I was able to follow. You navigated through the same darkness that I can move through. I observed the changeling using Dean's appearance."

"I suspect Cyndi was going to use those dreams to show you her murders," Dean said. "Let you inhabit one of those women as she killed them. To let you feel that sort of darkness firsthand. I suspect it would have forced you to seize control of the person you were dreaming as, letting your pride dominate them. To prove you were better than they were at their own life. Once you had a taste of it, you would fall further and further into sin. Cyndi would have led you into the darkness, the two of you united."

"And then the police got involved," I said. "And you. She was so shocked that you appeared at my apartment. And then... what? Why did she kiss me? Why did she try to seduce me so early? Did jealousy get the better of her? Did she panic?"

Dean shrugged and then groaned, pain crossing his face. His bandaged cheek winced. "It's hard to say. She didn't appear all that stable. I didn't know much about her. I just had a tip that a changeling was involved in something important."

"And now she's dead," I said, grief's pain spilling through me. "Why do I feel sorry about that? She tried to kill me. She was mad, but..."

Dean's strong hand pulled me towards him. I found myself slipping onto the bed and stretching out beside him. He released my hand to cup my face. His thumb stroked my cheekbone, brushing away a tear. "Because she was your friend. That's why you care."

"Just like I loved *him!*" I hissed. "And he hurt me, too. Is that my destiny? Is it the darkness inside my soul drawing me towards monsters?"

I gasped in shock as Dean's lips claimed mine, the bed creaking. I heard him groaning in pain while he kissed me, those hot lips working against mine. A flash of passion swept through me. I shuddered against him, unable to stop myself from caressing his bandaged chest. My touch skirted around his wounds as his tongue plunged into my mouth.

A wave of heat shot through me. This unbridled passion that my soul responded to. My pussy grew hotter and hotter. I wanted to mount him. To satiate myself. His kiss drowned me in passion.

Dean broke the kiss, leaving me panting. "Not everyone in your life is a monster, Kyrie."

I blinked my eyes as he groaned and settled his head back on the pillow. His eyes closed. I licked my lips, tasting him as I watched him. His breathing slowed as the pain faded from his face. Exhaustion and his wounds pressed him into sleep.

I stayed cuddled against him, enjoying the warmth of his body. Elizabeth slid her naked form with catlike grace onto the other side of him. She was careful not to touch his wounds as she stretched her arm across him so she could stroke my wrist with her gentle fingers.

"He saved me, too," she said.

Those words were so honest. Tears burned my eyes.

"Are you another... cambion?" I asked. "Like... a... I don't know, what are all the seven deadly sins?"

She shook her head. "I'm a familiar. A tortured soul plucked out of Hell and gifted to a person who'd pleased one of the seven mighty Lords." Her lips curled in disgust. "The one month I was with *him* was worse than being in Perdition. He beat me. Abused me, a substitute for something he'd lost. He was a wrath cambion, a berserker. And then Dean came.

"He was on the verge of falling into the darkness himself. But he saw how I was being treated and..." A huge smile crossed her lips. "He saved me. He wrenched my bond from that bastard and made me his. I've been so happy the last three months." She purred in delight as she rubbed her cheek against Dean's sleeping face.

"His heart is so empty." Her green eyes met mine. "He's searching for something. Maybe you could give it to him, Kyrie. I've seen how he looks at you. How he cares for you. I'm afraid that one day, the emptiness will consume him. He'll become like *him* or like your friend."

I shuddered. Could I end up like Cyndi? She used to be a good girl like me.

"Maybe..." I swallowed. This powerful ache beat in my heart. I didn't know Dean that well, but what I shared with him so far showed me he was a good man. "Maybe I can help fill his heart. I know mine is so empty. So lonely."

Elizabeth smiled at me as she rested her head on Dean's chest.

I pressed my cheek on his shoulder. I felt his warmth as I slipped into sleep. I wasn't afraid of my dreams. I knew that even if I fell into someone's thoughts, they wouldn't have to die.

There were monsters in this world, but I wasn't sleeping beside one of them.

~~*~~

Dean Walker

I opened my eyes, my arm throbbing. I was healing. The TV was on, Elizabeth perched before it in a cat-like crouch. Every familiar had an animal they instinctively gravitated towards. I smiled as I

130

watched her staring at the TV while beside me an angel slept.

Kyrie Hope.

Her last name felt like an omen. Maybe...

I glanced at the figure sleeping beside me. Kyrie looked at peace, her red hair spilling over the pillows, a few strands draped over her cheek. Her breasts rose and fell in the long t-shirt she wore. Memories of my last angel, my beautiful Terra, spilled through me.

As the pain stung my heart, I brushed the curls from Kyrie's face. A flush of crimson stained her cheek. She was a cambion, like me, but she possessed that same innocence that Terra had.

The innocence that had saved my soul from the darkness until she was taken from me.

I pushed down the grief.

The jingle of a commercial drew my attention. I glanced at the TV. Elizabeth had almost pressed her nose against the surface, her face just an inch away. If she was in her cat form, I knew her tail would be swishing and her ears twitching.

I admired her beauty for the next few minutes.

"Authorities are on the lookout for these two individuals," the news report said after the commercial ended and the evening news started. "Dean Walker and Kyrie Hope are wanted for questioning in the string of murders that culminated with the death of Officer Morgan and Cyndi Jakeman in her apartment early this morning. Police are unsure exactly what Kyrie's involvement with the crimes are, but she is believed to be an accomplice to Walker, aiding him in his murder spree."

I scowled at that. It would make things more difficult going forward. The changeling-bitch *would* have to frame me for her own murder along with those other girls'.

I sighed, doing the right thing wasn't supposed to be easy. A voice echoed through my memory. I could hear Terra now as clear as that day when she said, *"If it was easy, Dean, then everyone would do it. Then there wouldn't be any evil in the world. But that's what sin is: doing the easy thing. Being good takes struggle. And when you fight for something, when you strain to get it, you appreciate it.*

Treasure it."

I slipped my left arm beneath Kyrie's body. I flexed the fingers of my right hand, the pain in my arm fading. My body was healing. Kyrie whimpered as she snuggled tighter against me. Her arm slid across my chest. She held me tight, trusting me. At least now she knew who I was. I didn't want to see the fear of me in her eyes, like I had when I visited her apartment, ever again.

I smiled, remembering the way she'd spun around and pointed the gun at me. She was daring. Strong. A survivor. Together, I had a feeling we could make something. A future.

"Dean," Elizabeth said, turning her head. "I got a call from Grey. He says there is some activity with a cambion. You may like to check it out."

"Later," I said, "I need to sleep."

Elizabeth turned off the TV. She stood up, stretching her naked, lean body. Her small breasts ended at two taut points. "Good night." She sauntered towards the bed and slid in on the other side of Kyrie, hugging her. "I like her. She's good for you."

I smiled at my familiar. Then I let restorative sleep pull me down into dreams.

Chapter Eleven: The Incubus's Passion

Kyrie Hope

I didn't remember any special dreams when the shifting on the bed brought me awake. I opened my eyes, blinking to see Dean unwinding the splint from his arm. He had already removed the bandages from his broad chest. There were no wounds left. I blinked in shock, shifting, feeling a warmth hugging me from behind.

"How long was I asleep?" I asked, caressing his muscles.

"Ten hours," said Elizabeth as she pressed tighter against me. I felt the taut points of her firm breasts rubbing into my back through my nightshirt. This heat rippled through me.

"You're already healed?" I gasped, trying to ignore the heat while my hand slid over Dean's broad chest, feeling the warmth of him. The strength.

His piercing, blue eyes met mine. "The darkness does have its uses."

I shuddered, not wanting to think about my true nature. I bit my lip, this hunger swelling in my pussy. I breathed in that manly musk of his and caught the feminine perfume of Elizabeth mixed in it.

Cheeks burning, I said, "I think you... promised to do a few things to me. Before everything went bad."

A smile grew on his lips. It made my cheeks burn, along with the naughty glint in his blue eyes. "Right, right, a good girl needs to be spanked after just sucking my cock without even a date."

I nodded my head, so shocked by the strength of the lust gripping me. After everything we'd been through, we'd survived, we lived, and I wanted to celebrate that fact with my incubus. I didn't have to be afraid of him.

I could enjoy him.

My hands slid down his body, crossing his rippling abs as I went lower and lower. "I feel like I'm being such a naughty girl right now."

Elizabeth made a purring sound. Then her tongue licked my earlobe, sending a shiver down my body, caressing my nipples before it ended at my molten pussy. "You are a naughty girl," she husked. "I licked your pussy, and you didn't lick mine back."

"Oh, no," I said, shocked by how excited that made me. I'd never been into girls, but... I could feel the lust spilling off of Dean and into me, this dark passion that made me feel so wanton. "I should... fix that."

"Yes," Elizabeth moaned, squirming against me.

My hand went lower down Dean's abdomen, sliding beneath the blankets. I crossed his wiry pubic hair on my way to his throbbing cock. I gripped him, feeling the lust twitching through him.

I wanted to do such naughty things to him.

I stroked Dean's cock with an eagerness. I licked my lips, shivering. My lusts swelled in me. Elizabeth licked my ear again while her delicate finger stroked my arm, creeping up to the sleeve of my nightshirt. Dean grinned at me, and then he captured my lips in a molten kiss. I melted against him, my tongue dueling with his as my pussy soaked my poor panties.

"Let's get this off of you," purred Elizabeth. "It's not fair that you're the only one of us wearing clothes, Kyrie."

Not fair at all, I thought.

I shuddered as Elizabeth dragged my nightshirt up my body. She worked it slowly, pulling the cotton up my thighs as I kept kissing Dean. My hand stroked up and down his cock, his dick warm in my grip. His precum spilled out, coating my palm and lubing my pumping fist.

I gasped into the kiss then broke it to moan out, "Elizabeth!"

I shuddered at the hot contact of her lips as they kissed my upper thigh right at the swell of my rump. She licked up to my pantie line while she pulled my shirt higher. I shuddered at the naughty touch. She smooched across my rump as I squirmed. The hem of my top slid higher and higher. I whimpered as her tongue found the small of my back. My toes curled as she licked up my spine, her hands pushing my nightshirt higher.

Dean grinned at me, his dick throbbing in my grip. He stroked my face, his rough fingers sending fire shooting through me. "I feel your desire quivering. She's licking up your spine, right?"

I nodded my head, squirming as Elizabeth pushed the nightshirt higher and higher. Her tongue was wet and warm, almost feline in its playfulness. Sometimes she would kiss, quick smooches before she licked again. I groaned, this heat swelling out of my pussy.

"I've never had a threesome before," I groaned, my thumb rubbing over the crown of his dick. I spread his precum around the spongy tip as he grinned at me.

"You *are* being a naughty girl today," he told me as he leaned in for a kiss.

Before he claimed my lips, I moaned, "I need to earn that spanking."

His kissed me. His tongue thrust into my mouth as Elizabeth pushed the shirt over my breasts. They spilled out, and Dean's hand slid down to cup one. He kneaded it with strong fingers, his thumb sweeping out to brush my areola. My nipple.

Lightning shot down to my pussy.

Elizabeth kept licking up my spine higher and higher. I moaned into the kiss, trembling. It was so exciting. I drank in the lust spilling out of Dean and pouring into me. I didn't want to stop kissing him or stroking his cock.

However, we ran into a problem.

Elizabeth bunched my shirt beneath my armpits. I had to release Dean's cock and stop kissing him so she could pull off my top. I whimpered, Dean caressing my nipple as my nightshirt engulfed my head. It was off in a flash, the cloth fluttering off the side of the bed. My red hair fell around my face as Elizabeth pressed her naked body into my back, her nipples hard on my flesh.

This wasn't in a dream. This was real life. I had a woman rubbing against me. She nuzzled over my shoulder as I grabbed Dean's cock again. I turned my head. Elizabeth's lips met mine in a hot and hungry kiss. This was so unlike me, but it felt so right as our tongues danced together.

Like in my dream, my soul was feeding off the lust spilling off of Dean. I was responding to the incubus's desires. They merged into me, transforming my passion. It made this so exciting. I squirmed my thighs together, my pussy growing so hot as Elizabeth's soft and gentle lips kissed mine. She tasted so sweet.

"Gehenna's fires," growled Dean. "What a sight."

I shuddered, so glad I was pleasing him. My incubus...

I squealed into the kiss with Elizabeth as his lips engulfed my nub. He sucked on it, his tongue dancing around it. My pussy clenched while I spasmed. This trembling heat washed through me, waves that flowed out of my nipple every time he sucked. My panties grew stickier and stickier.

I broke the kiss with Elizabeth to gasp, "Oh, Dean, yes! You're going to take me to Paradise again!"

He sucked hard on my nipple.

"He takes every woman to Paradise," moaned Elizabeth, her hands sliding down my body as I squirmed, her breasts rubbing against my back. She reached my panties, her fingers slipping beneath the waistband. She tugged them down.

"Yes, yes, I want to go to Paradise!" I moaned as Elizabeth nibbled on my shoulder. My panties rolled down my rump then slid down my thighs.

I shuddered as I felt a strip of pubic hair rubbing into my ass. Elizabeth was waxed bikini style, a narrow line of silk leading down to her shaved pussy. Her pubic hairs tickled my rump. I loved the feel of her as she squirmed against me, my panties left bunched around my thighs. Elizabeth went back to kissing me over my shoulder, devouring my lips while Dean sucked on my hard nipple.

I stroked his cock faster, his dick throbbing in my grip. My pussy grew juicier and juicier. I couldn't believe we were doing this. This was... wild. Incredible. My tongue dueled with Elizabeth's, her nipples rubbing into my back, her ticklish landing strip caressing my rump.

She broke the kiss, her green eyes sparkling. "You want to really earn that spanking?"

I nodded my head. "What do you want me to do? I already promised to lick your pussy."

"Oh, we'll get to that," she promised. She licked my cheek. "Why don't we suck his cock together?"

I remembered that blowjob I gave Dean in the alley behind the club. I wanted to love him, to give him pleasure, unlike all those women who just wanted to take from him. I wanted to set myself apart from all those hordes of beautiful ladies who craved him. They just wanted him to eat their pussies and fuck their cunts until they came.

I wanted to love him. So did Elizabeth.

"Yes!" I moaned.

Dean popped his lips off my nipple, his dick twitching in my stroking hand. "You do want to be a bad girl. I like that."

"Good. It's your fault. You corrupted me."

"I'm just a wanderer," he said, feigning innocence. "I just drifted through the world. You're the one that wants to be naughty with me. You're the one who wants to do wicked things to me."

"Oh, don't you even pretend this isn't your fault," I said, a smile spreading on my lips. "You have to take full responsibility for turning me into a slut."

I shuddered at saying that word. Tyrone used to call me it. I hated when he did. Right now, my juicy pussy ached, and my heart pumped rapture through my veins. I wanted to be a slut. *Dean's* slut. No other guy's. The incubus had shown me something amazing. He'd shown me the true depths of my passion, all the pleasure my body could enjoy.

Now I was ready to give.

The hunger to suck Dean's cock swelled inside of me. I gripped his dick and found myself sliding down his body. My sensitive nipples grazed his chest on the way down. My lips crossed his broad pecs. I paused to flick his little nipple with my tongue.

He grinned at me, his blue eyes full of joy. "My devilish muse."

With feline grace, Elizabeth moved over both of us to end up on Dean's other side. Her small breasts hardly quivered as she pressed her mocha-brown figure against his body. Her hand joined mine on his dick, gripping higher up the shaft. Her green eyes flashed at me as she dove right for his cock. Her tongue flicked across the swollen crown and gathered up the precum.

Not wanting to be left out, I slid faster down Dean's body, my nipples aching as they dragged across his rippling abs and pressed into his hip. I ducked in, eager to share his dick with the familiar. My tongue brushed the side of the shaft above her brown fingers. I licked up and reached his crown, my tongue caressing his tip.

His dick throbbed in our grip.

"Damn," he moaned, "my devilish muse and my shadowy goddess together."

I grinned at the shadowy goddess. Elizabeth flashed a wicked smile back. I was close on guessing her name. No wonder she didn't object.

Then we attacked his dick together. Our tongues fluttered around the crown, caressing that spongy texture, gathering up the salty precum. My pussy clenched every time our nimble appendages brushed. Her lips caressed. Sometimes, it was almost like we were kissing each other around his cock. He groaned, his blue eyes watching us.

My red hair and Elizabeth's dark locks brushed each other, spilling about the other as we licked and nibbled and sucked on his dick. Both of us had our lips sealed around the side, making him gasp. His dick throbbed in my stroking grip. My hand would slide down to his thick bush then back up to brush Elizabeth holding his shaft.

"Damn, how did I get so lucky?" gasped Dean. "Gehenna's boiling fires!"

I winked at him. "When you do good deeds, they should be rewarded."

"Is that what this is?" he asked me, giving me a direct look.

My cheeks burned. Loving someone shouldn't be a reward. It should be something you wanted to give them because you want to make them feel good. When you started treating it like a transaction, you cheapened it.

"No," I admitted. "I'm doing this because... because I want to form a connection with you." I remembered something that Cyndi had said about how we all make connections with each other. That there were these threads, chains, ropes and more that bound us all together. She'd theorized that was how I was able to visit those women's dreams. I bet she was right. "I want to form something strong with you, Dean. It feels right. And I want to share it with Elizabeth." I stroked the familiar's black hair.

She flashed a wicked smile then engulfed Dean's cock.

"No fair!" I gasped as I watched her lips slide up and down on his dick.

"My shadowy goddess is a greedy one," Dean said, amusement in his voice. "Heaven's closed gates, but she knows how to suck cock."

I watched Elizabeth working her tight lips up and down his cock, my pussy clenching in envy. She looked so beautiful doing it. Her dark cheeks hollowed. Her green eyes were glossy with her passion. They met mine, hers burning with feline delight.

Her mouth popped off his dick, her hand pressing his cock towards me. "I don't mind sharing with you, Kyrie."

My fingers kept petting her hair as I leaned in and engulfed the tip of Dean's cock, tasting Elizabeth's saliva about him mixed with the salty precum.

He groaned as I sucked. I steeled my lips tight about his girth, my tongue dancing about his crown. I worked my head up and down, pleasing him, feeling his dick throb in my grip. My other hand clenched at Elizabeth's hair. She nuzzled then, licking at the boundary of my lips and Dean's shaft.

My pussy grew hotter and hotter as I pleasured him. My tongue danced around his cock as his precum spilled over my tongue. I wanted to keep sucking on him, to make him explode, but Elizabeth needed to please him, too. I didn't want to be selfish. She was willing to share.

I could, too. I could be just as amazing a participant in a threesome as I was one on one.

I shuddered at that pride swelling through me as I popped my mouth off Dean's dick. "Enjoy him, Elizabeth."

She winked at me.

"Fuck!" Dean groaned as his familiar swallowed his dick. "Having my devilish muse and my shadowy goddess together is worth all the pain."

I shuddered, feeling the truth of it.

Elizabeth and I loved him. We traded his dick back and forth, taking turns. I rejoiced every time I had his cock in my mouth, sucking on him, feeling his precum spilling over my tongue. Then this new joy filled me as I watched Elizabeth love him. I couldn't believe I could be happy with another woman blowing the guy I was falling in love with. But I was.

Maybe... maybe I was falling in love with her, too.

Dean growled louder and louder. His dick swelled in my hand. I could feel his lust thickening the air. I just knew that he was coming closer and closer to erupting. That he was almost to his exploding orgasm. I had a sense of what he wanted to see. What he wanted to experience.

"Elizabeth!" I moaned.

Her mouth popped off his dick. "Yes!" she purred. "Cum on our faces, Dean!"

We pressed our cheeks together, both our hands fisting up and down his dick. I stared up his body, his blue eyes filling with such passion. He grunted. He growled. His brawny chest swelled as he sucked in deep breaths.

"Heaven's fucking Providence, yes!" he growled. "I'll give you both such rapture. I will take you both to Paradise today. Every day. You're my women now!"

His cock erupted.

Dean's salty cum splattered across our faces. My mouth open, reveling in the incubus's seed. It splashed against the roof of my mouth before spilling over my tongue, my taste buds coming alive. I swallowed the creamy treat.

More and more of his passion painted us. His face twisted as he growled with his pleasure. My pussy clenched tight as I felt his lust in the air. It washed out of him in pulsing waves that were timed with the eruptions of his dick.

I dripped with cum.

It covered my features. And it covered hers.

Seeing Elizabeth's face covered in Dean's pearly passion sent hunger rushing through me. I did something I never imagined I ever would. I turned my head and nuzzled my lips into her cum-soaked cheek.

My tongue flicked out, gathering the salty spunk off her face.

I should've found it degrading, but instead, it made me feel hot. Wanton and wicked. I was sharing this naughty moment not only with the incubus with whom I was falling in love but his sexy familiar. Elizabeth and I were making him happy, Dean groaning loudly as I licked again. Elizabeth turned her head, her own tongue flicking out, gathering a line of dripping spunk off my cheek.

Tingles raced out of my wet pussy. My cunt clenched as we licked and lapped and bathed each other's face. I crossed her cheekbones. I gathered spunk that dribbled around her dainty nose. Her tongue flicked across my chin and lapped at the nape of my neck. That salty treat melted on my tongue. He tasted so amazing.

Our lips met.

Elizabeth thrust her cum-coated tongue into my mouth. We were sharing his jizz now. Our tongues dueled together, passing the salty delight back and forth. I felt Dean watching us, grinning. His lust quivered around us, caressing our souls. I groaned, my own desires swelling in the depths of my pussy.

My hands grabbed Elizabeth's shoulders. I pushed her back as we kissed. I pressed her down onto the bed and slid atop her. I straddled her, my silky bush rubbing into her stomach, our breasts meeting. Our tongues dueled as I squirmed atop her, my nipples sliding over her soft yet firm breasts. That strange dichotomy made me shudder. Our nipples kissed, lightning shooting down to my pussy.

"Gehenna's boiling flames, but you two are beautiful. Two angels. Heaven's pearly gates, you two inspire me."

I shuddered, really wanting to inspire him. And I knew how as I remembered my promise to Elizabeth. I broke our kiss and nibbled my lips across her chin. I nuzzled down to her throat. She purred, that feline passion rumbling out of her vocal cords as I kissed down to the nape of her neck.

My hands caressed her sides as I smooched lower and lower, reaching her collarbone. My nipples pressed her soft flesh. She felt so different from the hard masculinity of Dean.

His opposite.

I loved her sleek delight. I kissed lower and lower, my pale fingers cupping her dark breasts. I squeezed those firm, little titties. My lips climbed her right one. Elizabeth's purring grew louder and louder as I approached her nipple, my own hard nubs throbbing against her satin-sleek belly.

I reached the edge of her areola, the texture of her skin changing. My tongue swirled out, dancing around her nipple. Then my lips engulfed her nub. I sucked hard, reveling in the gasp of pleasure bursting from her lips.

"That's it," Dean growled. "Love her, my devilish muse. So

beautiful, Kyrie. Both of you. Goddamn, how did I get so lucky to have you both in my life? You're fallen angels. I have to return you both to Paradise."

My pussy clenched at his words. I sucked hard at Elizabeth's nipple, giving her pleasure. I loved her nub while my fingers kneaded her firm breasts, squeezing them, teasing her. Pussy juices soaked through my bush and trickled down my thighs.

I was so wet.

How wet was Elizabeth?

Aching to find out, I abandoned her nipple and kissed down her body. I smooched around her torso, my lips loving her silky skin. My nipples ached as I dragged my breasts lower. My tits reached her mostly-shaved pubic mound. My left breast grazed her landing strip; her wiry hair caressed my tit. I moved lower, my breast sliding past her pubic mound and spilling between her thighs. I felt the wet heat of her pussy on my breast for a moment, my lips aching to nuzzle her there.

I smooched lower and lower down her mound while Dean maneuvered behind me. I felt his eyes on me. I groaned, my lips reaching her pubic mound, nuzzling at the landing strip. Her pubic hairs caressed my lips.

"Yes, yes, Kyrie," she moaned, her hands sweeping up her sleek, dark body to grab her small tits.

"Mmm, what a naughty slut," growled Dean. "Such a bad, bad girl. Teasing my familiar."

SMACK!

I gasped at the first stinging spank landed on my ass. The burning heat shot through me, melting down to my pussy. I moaned, quivering, loving it. I wiggled my hips, aching for another blow. At the same time, my lips kissed down Elizabeth's landing strip. I nuzzled into the top folds of her pussy, tasting her spicy musk.

Another woman's pussy juices stained my lips.

SMACK!

Dean's strong hand landed on my left butt-cheek this time. The stinging pain melted through my rump to my pussy. My snatch clenched as I drank in the sensation. I whimpered. My tongue fluttered out, licking through Elizabeth's folds. Her labia caressed me. I gathered up her spicy cream, the flavor bursting to life on my tongue. I licked again and again, in love with her flavor.

"Spank the bad girl, Dean!" moaned Elizabeth. "She's licking my pussy!"

SMACK!

I groaned into Elizabeth's snatch, the pain enhancing the ache in the depths of my femininity. It swelled my need to be fucked. I whimpered and jammed my tongue deep into Elizabeth's twat, swirling around against her silky walls. My own cream dripped down my thighs.

"Fuck the bad girl!" moaned Elizabeth. "Fuck her naughty, little cunt. She wants it. She's my owner! She wants you to love her! Take her to Paradise!"

"Yes!" I moaned into her snatch.

SMACK!

I savored the fourth spark of pain. I arched my back and thrust my ass at him. I had no idea that agony could become rapture. Being spanked by my incubus sent such lust through me. I was so horny. I needed my man to be in me.

His cock buried into my pussy in a single thrust.

I groaned into Elizabeth's snatch as his girth filled me. He spread me open wide, plunging into my sopping cunt. His balls smacked into my clit, sparks showering through my twat. My eyes rolled back in my head.

My incubus was incredible.

"Dean, Dean, yes!" I moaned. "Fly me to Paradise as I send Elizabeth howling to Nirvana."

SMACK!

"Naughty girl," Dean growled as he pumped his dick in and out of my pussy.

"She is such a naughty girl," moaned Elizabeth as my tongue plundered her spicy pussy.

I was. And loving it.

My hips swayed back and forth, rotating my pussy around Dean's dick slamming in and out of my twat. My snatch clenched down on Dean, increasing the friction. The pleasure. I reveled in this moment. Heat built and built in me. My eyes fluttered as he buried into me, my breasts swaying.

I groaned as my hips worked in circles, stirring his dick around inside of my pussy. My incubus took me hard. Fast. His crotch smacked into my stinging ass. It reminded me of those wicked spankings. I felt like such a naughty slut, compelling me to press my face into Elizabeth's shaved pussy.

Her hot folds caressed my lips and cheeks. Her spicy musk filled my every inhalation. She gasped and groaned, her dark, creamy thighs clenching about my face. My fiery hair spilled over her skin as I feasted on her. I flicked my tongue up, brushing her clit.

My own ached as Dean's heavy balls smacked into my bud over and over.

"I seem to recall a naughty girl saying I could do wicked things to her," growled Dean.

I gasped as he ripped his cock out of my pussy. I suddenly felt so empty. I had been coming closer and closer to my orgasm, nearer and nearer to Paradise, but now it was fading. I whimpered into Elizabeth's pussy. I was about to lift my head and beg Dean to slam back into me when the wet tip of his dick pressed between my buttcheeks.

Found my asshole.

My eyes widened as I remembered our flirty conversation. I had implied I'd let him fuck me up the ass. I never, ever, let Tyrone do that to me. No matter how much he hurt me, I refused to give him that satisfaction. I did it out of pride. The one thing I wouldn't surrender to that bastard.

"Fuck my asshole!" I cried out, eager to give it to Dean.

I sucked hard on Elizabeth's clit as Dean pressed his cock against my asshole. He pressed against me. My sphincter widened, stretching and stretching to engulf his pussy-lubed cock. I gasped into Elizabeth's clit, sucking with such passion as Dean penetrated my bowels.

I groaned with every inch of his dick sliding into me. His girth spread open my velvety sheath. It was a pleasure, unlike anything I'd ever experienced. I shuddered, my asshole squeezing down around his dick, clenching to him as he went deeper and deeper into me. I shuddered as he speared into my depths, filling my bowels with his hard cock.

"I think the naughty girl's into anal," purred Elizabeth, her hips undulating, smearing her hot pussy lips against my mouth.

"I think she is, too," Dean said, his strong hands stroking up my sides, sending ripples of heat shooting down to my pussy.

Both my holes clenched, my bowels gripping his dick, my pussy aching to be filled. Dean was so deep in my bowels. I whimpered, rubbing my face into Elizabeth's juicy snatch. I reveled in this moment, loving every second of it. My incubus's dick was in my asshole. I had surrendered everything to him.

He drew back, my bowels gripping his cock. I groaned and drank in the velvety friction. When there was only the tip still in me, he rammed back into me. He slammed in hard, this knifing heat that speared deep into my bowels. His balls smacked my taint and the upper folds of my pussy.

"Gehenna's fires!" I cried out, using one of Dean's strange swearwords. "Oh, fuck, you're in my asshole!"

"Such a naughty girl," Dean growled as he drew back again. "Elizabeth, you should wash out that dirty mouth of hers."

Elizabeth giggled, her green eyes flashing at me down her body.

She grabbed my fiery hair and pulled my face tight against her pussy. She ground against me as Dean pounded my asshole. I loved the bliss melting down to my pussy with his every thrust. My cunt drank it in as my tongue fluttered through Elizabeth's folds.

I devoured her spicy passion, licking it up, savoring the flavor of it. It spilled over my tongue and coated my lips. I gulped down her cream as I plunged my tongue into her feverish flesh again and again.

The three of us were moaning, groaning. Dean slammed his dick deep into my bowels while I moaned into Elizabeth's juicy snatch. The three of us were sharing this pleasure. This wonderful rapture.

I squeezed my bowels around his dick as my orgasm swelled inside of me. The friction of his dick plunging into me was enough to build my climax. I couldn't believe it.

I would cum from anal.

Pussy juices dripped down my thighs, my pussy on fire. I shuddered, bucking back into his strokes. His dick slammed into me, his crotch spanking my rump. I groaned and flicked my tongue in and out of Elizabeth's pussy.

"Gehenna's sinful flames!" gasped Elizabeth, her small breasts quivering. "Kyrie! You're amazing! Yes!"

A flood of her spicy juices filled my mouth. Her cream spilled across my tongue. I drank down her cream while realizing I had made her cum. I took her to Nirvana like I'd promised. She spasmed on the bed, gasping, moaning, receiving the same pleasure she'd given me in that dream.

My bowels clamped down hard on Dean's thrusting cock. As I licked up Elizabeth's juices, I found myself coming closer and closer to my own explosion. The burning delight of Dean's cock plunging into my bowels mixed with the pride that I'd made Elizabeth cum. It swelled my climax. The pleasure quivered through me. I gave her such rapture, and now I would give it to Dean.

"Gehenna's dark flames!" growled Dean. "Devilish muse! What are you doing to my cock? Goddamn, you're amazing Kyrie."

"So are you, Dean! I'm almost in Paradise!" I howled.

I licked through Elizabeth's pussy. More and more of her juices flooded out of her as she kept cumming. Dean slammed to the hilt inside of me. I gasped as his dick filled my bowels. I groaned, my asshole clenching about his girth. The burning friction melted into my pussy.

I came.

My bowels spasmed around his dick, celebrating this moment. He thrust hard into me. Dean filled me. I whimpered and groaned, the waves of heat washing out of my convulsing pussy melting my brain. Stars danced before me as I plunged my tongue deep into Elizabeth's pussy.

It was magnificent. Amazing. I came from getting fucked up the ass by my incubus.

"I love you, Dean!" I howled.

"Cum in her, my owner!" moaned Elizabeth.

My bowels spasmed about Dean's plunging cock. Every thrust sent new waves of rapture splashing through me. It was an incredible pleasure to enjoy. I moaned into Elizabeth's spicy pussy. I drank down her juices as my orgasm burned through me.

"Gehenna's fucking flames!" exclaimed Dean. He buried to the hilt in my asshole.

I felt the first spurt of his hot cum into my bowels. I shuddered, reveling in the wicked treat. I trembled on the bed, moaning into Elizabeth's twat. My asshole spasmed around his dick, milking my incubus dry. This was such an incredible delight. Such an amazing treat. I lifted my head, wild joy burning through me.

The last two days had been both terrible and wonderful. I felt a fluttering guilt that I was enjoying myself right now, but I had found something special with Dean and Elizabeth. Something amazing.

"I want to join you," I moaned. "I want to be a wanderer with you. You came here for a reason, didn't you? You're trying to stop this evil that destroyed Cyndi."

"Yes!" he growled, his dick twitching in my asshole.

"I want to help." I declared. "I have powers. I can use them."

He nodded.

"And I want your cock in my pussy right now," moaned Elizabeth. "I want you to fuck me while Kyrie rides my face."

That sounded really kinky. "Let me get something to wash off his dick."

Elizabeth shook her head. "I like it dirty. Don't forget, I'm still a familiar. I came from Hell."

My asshole clenched down on Dean's cock. Ass to pussy? It was the filthiest thing I'd ever heard. This strange rush went through me.

I wanted to watch that.

~~*~~

Dean Walker

I groaned as I pulled my still-hard dick out of Kyrie's asshole. There were definite advantages to being a half-devil. My mother's lusty darkness kept my dick hard. I breathed in, inhaling more than just the air and the feminine musk perfuming it. I breathed in both Elizabeth's and Kyrie's passion. Their lusts fed my soul. So long is it was willingly given to me, I didn't risk the darkness consuming me. If I ever lost control, if I ever *took*...

Kyrie would help. She and Elizabeth would keep that from happening. They were both amazing. I never thought I could love after losing Terra, but...

I smiled as Kyrie crawled up the bed, my cum trickling down her butt-crack and across her taint to mat down her fiery bush. Elizabeth licked her lips in eager excitement. Kyrie straddled my familiar's face, lowering her bright, red bush towards Elizabeth's dark lips.

My familiar grabbed Kyrie's pale thighs, pulling her down. Kyrie shuddered, grinding her pussy on Elizabeth's mouth. I could feel the joy Elizabeth received at licking up my cum fresh from Kyrie's asshole and mixed in with the redhead's pussy juices. I also felt the delight spilling through Kyrie body as Elizabeth feasted on her.

"You're really going to fuck your cock into her straight from my ass?" Kyrie moaned as I moved between Elizabeth's spread-wide thighs.

"I'm still a half-devil," I growled. "There has to be *an* outlet for the darkness in me."

Kyrie shuddered, pleasure spilling across her face. She grabbed my dick and guided it towards Elizabeth's shaved pussy. I felt the quivering excitement coming from my familiar, eager for my dirty cock to plunge into her pussy. I groaned as Kyrie pressed me against Elizabeth's hot, silky, juicy folds.

"Fuck her hard," Kyrie moaned. "Give her such nasty pleasure."

I saw that pride shining in Kyrie's green eyes. I grinned at her, seizing her red hair in a tight grip and pulling her to my lips. As I kissed Kyrie, I thrust into my other woman's pussy. My dick plunged deep into Elizabeth's tight, juicy snatch. Her flesh clenched around me, buffing my cock clean of Kyrie's asshole.

Kyrie whimpered into my lips, her tongue playing with mine buried in her mouth. I groaned, drawing back my hips. My cock drank in the silky delight of Elizabeth's pussy. I thrust deep, her tight sheath polishing my cock. Pleasure rippled from the tip of my sensitive dick and melted down towards my balls.

They smacked heavily into Elizabeth's taint.

"Yes, yes, yes," Elizabeth moaned into Kyrie's pussy. "My owner! By Gehenna's dark flames, clean your dick in my pussy. Let me serve you in every way!"

Her moans filled the air while her lust spilled through the room. It washed over me, brimming with her delight. She loved serving me. She squeezed her pussy down around my dick, her hips wiggling from side to side, washing her cunt around my dirty shaft.

I thrust hard into her, wanting to give my familiar as much rapture as I gave Kyrie.

My right hand found Kyrie's tit and my left cupped Elizabeth's small breast. I squeezed them both—Kyrie's was plumper, Elizabeth's firmer. I tweaked their nipples, both moaning, Kyrie into my mouth and Elizabeth into hot pussy.

I pleased both my women, fucking Elizabeth hard, kissing Kyrie with passion. I played with their nipples. Their lust brimmed throughout the room. They gave me this pleasure. I could feel their climaxes building in the air. Their passion. Their love. That darkness in my soul couldn't devour me so long as I had them. I don't know what Providence led me to find Kyrie and save her from the machinations of the Lords of Hell, but I was thrilled.

I would love her. Protect her. Cherish her.

I wouldn't lose her like I had Terra.

I broke the kiss, growling, "Together, we're going to hold back the darkness!"

"Yes, yes, yes!" Kyrie moaned. "The three of us!"

My thrusts grew harder, faster. I plunged deep into Elizabeth's cunt, churning up her passion. Her pussy squeezed around me, the silky embrace swelling my orgasm. I felt both their climaxes growing inside of them. Kyrie squirmed and groaned, her round breasts jiggling in my squeezing grip. Her back arched, her fiery hair dancing about her shoulders.

That heavenly ache built at the tip of my cock. Elizabeth's pussy was taking me to Paradise. I thrust hard into her, savoring every silky inch of her sheath. The friction transformed into ecstasy. It spilled through me, tightening my balls. The bliss swelled and swelled in them.

I kissed Kyrie again, trembling on the verge of my eruption.

I drew back my cock through Elizabeth's pussy, her cunt clenching down hard. She whimpered. I could feel her lust trembling through her soul. She drank in the bliss of my dick thrusting into her. The pleasure of it quivered through her. Kyrie groaned as I slammed back into her, burying into the depths of her sheath.

I felt the moment her orgasm triggered.

I fed on the lust spilling out of her, that hot passion that burst from her soul. Her pussy spasmed around my cock, rippling and massaging my girth. She moaned out in gasping passion into Kyrie's snatch, shuddering on the bed as her twat convulsed around my dick. Her passion filled the room.

She set off my devilish muse.

A heartbeat after Elizabeth's orgasm, rapture detonated inside of Kyrie. She moaned into our kiss, her tongue thrusting into my mouth as her pleasure rippled through her. I drank it in, delighting in devouring her passion. She flooded Elizabeth's mouth with her sweet juices. I groaned into the kiss, feeding on both of them. On their willing desire.

Their passion pressed down the darkness in my soul. Just like Terra's love had.

I drove my cock to the hilt in Elizabeth's pussy. I joined my two lovers in Paradise.

I broke the kiss with Kyrie, howling, "Gehenna's black flames!"

My cum pumped fast and hard into Elizabeth's pussy. I flooded her with my jizz. I filled her to the brim with my passion. My balls ached as they unloaded every salty drop of my lust. I reveled in giving my familiar my seed after she fed my soul. My cum filled my lover's pussy. My familiar came harder, groaning her passion into Kyrie's twat.

"Dean, Dean!" moaned Kyrie. She slumped forward, hands gripping my broad shoulders. Her green eyes twinkled. "I think... I think I'm falling in love with you."

I kissed her again, loving her back.

As Elizabeth's pussy milked my cock, I reveled in this moment. The three of us would hold back the darkness. We would rebel against those bastards down and in Hell. They wanted to use us, to twist the evil in us and wield it towards their own diabolical purpose. None of us were born from love, but what we gained from our human parents would give us the strength to defy Hell's machinations.

We collapsed together in panting passion. I hugged both my women to me, holding them tight, and I knew we could face what came next together. Hell had gambled today, thinking they could corrupt my sweet Kyrie.

They'd failed.

But there were others out there, other half-devils that the Lords of Hell sought to corrupt. I would save those other souls, defy the Infernal Dukes,, and make them pay for murdering my Terra.

Epilogue

In the austere autopsy room, everything was stainless steel or white-painted walls. Cold and lifeless as the body lying on an exam table. A woman: young, pretty. Her blonde hair fell lank about her still face, her body pale, life fled from her. Numerous bullet wounds and a deep stab to her chest marred the perfection of her flesh.

The soul animating Cyndi Jakeman had fled, pulled down to hell.

An infernal scream rippled through the exam room. Flares of devilish reds and agonizing oranges reflected off of every metal surface. The screams of the damned reached a piercing screech then died in the wake of a man stepping into reality. He appeared dapper in his crisp, black suit and fedora. His hair had a silvery-gray quality, his face distinguished, handsome. He was a man of means and wealth. A man who'd gained every status that society valued.

He adjusted a cufflink as he stared down at Cyndi's corpse. He shook his head. "Your father will not be pleased." A smile crossed the devil's lips. "Not one bit."

An angelic choir sang. Radiant light burst within the autopsy room. The devil winced, raising his hand against the heavenly glare. A figure stepped out, a man who could be a twin to the devil, dressed in a white suit. His hair was iron gray and combed back. He didn't look so much as dapper as powerful; a warrior who'd donned the diplomat's guise in place of armor.

The angel fixed his gaze. "Sterling."

The devil, going by Sterling at the present, nodded his head. "Chaumel. How wonderful to see you."

The angel snorted. "Your daughter didn't fall to corruption. She still has goodness in her soul. Cyndi failed."

"And paid for it," Sterling answered. "But do not worry. *Our* little deal is still in effect. My daughter is just where she needs to be."

"I thought we needed her to fall!" growled the archangel,

righteous anger boiling across his handsome features. For a moment, the echo of ethereal wings flashed behind him, haloed by a golden brilliance.

"That's what's so amazing about sin," the devil said. "We always get another chance at temptation. Things are already in motion. Your son-in-law—"

"Dean is not my son-in-law!" the angel snarled. "He destroyed my daughter. Defiled her!"

"She's not *wholly* destroyed." Sterling smiled. It didn't touch his scarlet eyes. "As I was saying, Dean has already been drawn to his next impotent crusade. My daughter will go with him. She's a prideful creature. You shall see. When she falls... you will get everything that you crave, Chaumel."

The End of Book One

About the Author

Reed James is a thirty year-old guy living in Tacoma, WA. "I love to write, I find it freeing to immerse myself in a world and tell its stories and then share them with others." He's been writing naughty stories since high school, furiously polishing his craft, and finally feels ready to share his fantasies with the world.

"I love writing about women who want to be a little (or a lot) naughty, people expressing their love for each other as physically and kinkily as possible, and women loving other women. Whether it's a virgin experiencing her/his first time or a long-term couple exploring the bounds of their relationships, it will be a hot, erotic story!"

You can find Reed on the internet at the following places:

Twitter: https://twitter.com/NLPublications
Facebook: https://www.facebook.com/reed.james.9231
Blog: http://blog.naughtyladiespublications.com/wp
Newsletter: http://eepurl.com/4nlN5

Printed in Great Britain
by Amazon